TWO STATUES

TWO STATUES

Brian Kennelly

 SAINT BENEDICT+PRESS
Charlotte, North Carolina

ISBN: 978-1-61890-390-7

Cover design by Chris Pelicano.

Printed and bound in the United States of America.

SAINT BENEDICT✝PRESS
Charlotte, North Carolina
2012

To Tina, my companion on this adventure from sunrise to sunset, may the adventure continue with our growing family.

To my parents, for providing me this life through support and sacrifice.

To Our Lord, for all these blessings he hath bestowed.

1

September 5th, 1995

AS I stand outside this small, stone church, I can't help but wonder about all that led to this moment. It isn't often that a Southern, black man born to Methodist parents finds himself outside a Catholic church, standing in the cool, gusty winds of a Rhode Island harbor town. But that's where I am.

I watch as strangers walk past the red, oak doors and into the church, wondering how they were affected by what took place here. I don't know many of these people, other than the two priests. They both glance at me, and I at them. We smile. We know how *we* were affected. Their side of the story runs different from mine, but we're all here today to honor what happened.

I had a front seat view to the strange phenomenon that occurred three years ago in the early fall of 1992. But my place wasn't here in Rhode Island; it was down south, where the winds aren't so cold and fast. The marshes and dunes of Edisto Island, South Carolina also held witness to what happened, in a different sort of way but also the same, and that's where

I better journey back to if I aim to find the seed this story grew from.

In 1988 I lost my brother Earl to lung cancer. I'd told him a dozen times to kick the tobacco, but he'd never listen to his baby brother, and besides, I was smoking those lung darts too. We'd both lived in Gable, South Carolina our whole lives. It was a pleasant place with more barns than stoplights. I'd always been one for dirt roads instead of paved ones, so I didn't mind the slow pace of life. But I grew restless after losing Earl. Home didn't seem like home anymore. It's funny how that happens. Home is supposed to be a place, but it's really more about the people.

I decided I needed to see the ocean on a daily basis. That seemed like the best medication for a lonely man meeting the dawn of his later years, so in my mid-sixties I packed up and moved down to Edisto Island. I found a small house not a ways from the water, leaning toward the crashing waves like the tide had been pulling on it for years. If I were being generous I'd call it a beach cottage, but if I were being honest it was more of a beach shack. When I moved in it was clear the home hadn't been inhabited in some years. Cobwebs, dust and mold seemed to be the only residents in the last decade or so. Rust gathered on the tin roof like sand on a beach, and the front door was lost to the rot and needed replacing real bad-like. But the home was stationed beyond the oak tree woodland of the island, where the trees ended and gave way to the beach. It was far enough away from the tourists and families with summer homes who'd invaded the island like termites to a barn. In this secluded corner, you could still hear the rustling of tree branches and still let the crashing waves put you to sleep. I

would eventually learn the locals joked it was the moss draping the trees which hid us from the tourists, like a blanket of
privacy provided by Mother Nature herself. So I didn't mind
so much the condition of my new home; the setting suited me
just fine.

It only took a few hours to move in. A bed, a table, a couch,
some chairs and lamps, and a few pairs of overalls weren't hard
to unload. But don't feel sorry for me; not owning much can
sometimes be a blessing rich folk never know of. I settled in
on my back porch right as the sun was departing for the night,
with a cigarette and Budweiser, content with my solitude until
the Grim Reaper came calling in his black cloak. I had all the
entertainment I needed as I watched the pelicans dive into the
sea in search of dinner. But to my right, in the direction of the
only other house in the area, I heard the slam of a screen door.
I looked over and saw an older, white man strolling down the
steps of his back porch, holding a tackle box and two fishing
poles, with a young, yellow lab nipping at his heels closer than
a shadow. They walked across his backyard and into mine, just
two patches of grass overrun by sand and bits of seashell. As
they approached, I looked out over the ocean and pretended
not to notice my new neighbor and his dog.

He stopped just a few feet short of my porch. "Want to
go fishin'?"

The pitch of his voice was deep, but soft. I turned around.
"Oh, hi there. I'm Buck Washington. You live next door?"

I stood up and moved down the steps to shake his hand.
After all, if he was nice enough to come over and invite me on
a fishing trip, I should at least be cordial before I turned him
down.

He gripped my hand and nodded at his dog. "Walter Henderson, but call me Walt, and this here's Sam. Want to go fishin'?"

I looked him up and down, taking in his drooping face, graying hair, and faded clothes. He sized me up as well as I stood before him bare-chested, with my favorite pair of overalls hanging on my shoulders. He was white and I black, but I could tell neither of us gave that any mind.

"Ya' know, Walt," I said as I rubbed Sam on the head and let him lick my hand. "That's mighty noble of you to invite me, but I'm not really a fisherman. Never really had an interest in it."

"All right," he replied, as if he already knew what my answer would be. "We'll be down yonder in the cove if you change your mind. Nice little tide pool develops this time a' day."

He and Sam disappeared past the dunes leading to the water as I went back and sat on my rocker. Glancing behind me at my mostly empty and dark house, I wondered why I shouldn't take the chance to sit with my toes in the sand and enjoy the salty air rising off the sea. I'd told Walt I never had an interest in fishing, but that couldn't have been further from the truth. A few minutes and an empty beer later, I had an unexpected change of heart. I kicked off my shoes and followed the path they'd taken. After rounding a bend in the island, I saw the pair sitting before the water with their backs to me. When I reached them, Walt didn't even turn 'round; he just held out his extra pole, and I took it from him. Judging by his wagging tail, Sam seemed glad I had changed my mind.

Walt, Sam, and I fished for an hour that day. We didn't

say a word to each other and we didn't catch a fish; just sat on a small bank of sand before a gentle tide pool. Night fell around us, making it easier to see the glow of the fireflies and the sprinkling of the stars against the black sky. When it was time to go we walked back to our separate homes.

I drifted off to sleep with ease that night as the crickets sang their melodies outside. I had one of the deepest sleeps I can recall that first night in Edisto, but at the break of daylight I was awoken by something I wasn't expecting.

Music.

But not music from a stereo. It had that distinct sound live music has, the way it tickles your ear with a little more meaning. I climbed off my rickety, single-mattress bed and stumbled to the window. I rubbed my eyes to get rid of the blurriness. When I had gathered my wits, I finally saw the source of the music: Walter Henderson was outside on the beach, sitting in a chair and playing a violin, with his dear dog Sam lying next to him on the sand, as still as a figure in a painting. It took a few moments for it all to register. I thought for a second I may have been dreaming, but I surely wasn't. I sank back down on my bed and leaned against the wall. Walt's music drifted around me, as peaceful a sound as I'd ever heard.

I didn't know it at the time, but I was listening to a man speak with God.

2

September 5th, 1995

A S I stand outside this small, stone church, I can't help but
wonder about all that led to this moment. Many of the
people walking past the red, oak doors and into the narthex
glance at me and smile, though as a visiting priest I know very
few of them. Eventually, I catch the eye of Buck Washington
and exchange a nod. I can't help but smile myself as I recall his
Southern charm. The paths which led us to this Rhode Island,
harbor town were as different as our accents, but those paths
converged today because of what happened in the fall of 1992.

If there is one thing I know that the common man over-
looks, it is that priests are not born priests. There was a time
when I was simply Paul Moore; I chose to become *Father* Paul
Moore over ten years ago, in the midst of my early twenties.
But just as we are not born into our calling, we may also not
die with this white collar around our neck. I once assumed in
my youth, perhaps ignorantly, that a priest would never lose
sight of his faith.

Three years ago I learned how wrong I could be.

I awoke in the pitch of night to a commotion coming from the front of my house. For the last five years I had lived on the campus grounds of Assumption College in Worcester, Massachusetts with my friend and colleague, Father Peter Davis. It was just the two of us in the one-story home, so I assumed the noise was coming from him. At least I hoped it was him and not a stranger.

I threw on my robe and opened the door to my bedroom. Turning toward the front of the house, I saw Peter standing in the open doorway, a knapsack thrown over his shoulder and dressed in a way I had never seen. He wore sneakers, jeans, and a gray, hooded sweatshirt. When he saw that I had woken up, his expression dropped. He suddenly looked guilty of something.

"What on earth are you doing, Peter? Where are you going?"

He shook his head. "I . . . I don't know."

"You don't know? What are you talking about? Come back inside."

"I can't, Paul."

"What do you mean you can't?"

"I mean, I don't know. Can we just sit outside? Go on a walk or something? I need to get some air."

"Why do you need a duffle bag to get some air?"

He didn't answer.

"Just hold on. Let me get some shoes and clothes on."

I changed quickly and when I returned he was sitting on our front stairs. He rose and together we turned down the street toward the main part of campus. We both knew where we were going. We'd often follow the same path on daily walks around the school, cutting through the campus buildings and circling around the church before coming back up around to our house. The night was dark and cold and it was clear summer was over as the silence between us settled in the autumn wind gusts. I felt that he should speak first but it didn't appear that he would.

"What's going on, Peter?"

We had taken several steps before he answered.

"I have to get out of here, Paul."

"Out of Worcester?"

"Out of this life. This isn't for me anymore."

I wished I could've said this admission came as a shock, but it didn't. As Peter's best friend I could easily see the change that had overtaken him in the last months. He was not the same priest I met five years ago when we both arrived on campus to begin our teaching duties. Just last week I had found him passed out in his bed with an empty handle of vodka sitting on the floor. He was so sick the next day I was forced to replace him at the early morning, student Mass. It was the lowest I had ever seen him, until perhaps tonight.

"I tried talking to you last week but you wouldn't open up. I don't know what you're going through but I want to help. Why would you try to leave in the middle of the night without talking to me?"

"Shame, I guess. It's not like I want to feel like this."

"Where were you even going?"

"Don't know; anywhere but here." He reached into his pocket and pulled out crumpled cash folded over and held together with a rubber band. "I've been stealing this out of the Poor Box in church for the last two months. I was going to buy a Greyhound ticket to wherever this would get me." My jaw dropped. "Save your lecture," he mumbled, returning the money to his pocket.

"What's happened?" I asked.

"It's complicated."

"You know you can tell me no matter what it is."

He took a deep breath. "Do you remember our mission trip to Costa Rica this past summer?"

I hesitated, confused. "Yes, of course I do."

"I met a child there, a little girl, probably five or six years-old. I learned on our first day she was an orphan. When I tried to find out what happened to her parents, I regretted it. It turns out her father was just a stranger who'd raped her mother, and her mother had killed herself shortly after giving birth to her child. I don't know why the mother committed suicide, but I assume it was because her life had become unbearable. I know the girl hadn't eaten in days, and when we left I had no reason to believe she would survive another month."

We crossed the street and curved around the Philosophy and Theology building where our classes were taught. I peered up to the second floor window to the office Peter and I shared, taking note of the small statue of the Virgin Mary which sat perched on our windowsill. I liked looking at it throughout the day.

We circled the building and cut through a courtyard. My mind was racing back to our mission trip and whether or not I had met this little girl.

"I'm sorry, Peter, I don't understand. What does this little girl have to do with you picking up and leaving in the middle of the night?"

"Nothing, really. I guess I just saw something in her. I started to wonder how God could let that happen, how he could let a little girl have that kind of life."

"Is this really what you want to talk about? As priests we've both had hundreds of conversations with distraught people, trying to explain how God brings goodness out of the tragedies of this world. I've heard you counsel people brilliantly on these matters. Why are you all of a sudden questioning God after meeting a little, orphaned girl?"

"Relax, Paul. To answer your question, I don't want to talk about this. I'm in no mood for a philosophical conversation about suffering and God's intentions."

Up ahead I could see the silhouette of the church steeple as it rested flush against the moonlit sky. We walked toward it blindly and without thought; we had made this walk a thousand times.

"What do you want to talk about then?" I asked.

He hesitated, seemingly lost in thought for a moment.

"I'm not sure why I became a priest, Paul. If I'm being perfectly honest, I sort of fell into it by necessity rather than by choosing. I've never really told you much about my past because there are some things there I'd just as soon forget. You wouldn't believe what I could tell you."

"Try me."

"Are you sure you want to hear this?"

"Positive."

He nodded, but hesitated again, deciding if he truly wanted to let me in.

"After I turned eighteen, I found myself out on the streets. My family . . ." he paused, "let's just say they weren't the most loving people, so I ran away from home. This sounds pathetic, but I think it took about two weeks for me to fall into a world of drugs. I was too weak to fight temptations at that point in my life. I slept for a whole month in a crack house, without a single possession to my name except the clothes on my back and the drug pipe in my pocket. It was a dangerous place but it put a roof over my head for a while, until the cops came one night and I was on the run."

As he spoke, I struggled to digest everything. Hearing this made my best friend seem more like a stranger in only a matter of seconds. I couldn't imagine Peter, the man and priest I had come to know so well, living through such horrid experiences.

"I began to frequent a few homeless shelters from time to time," he went on, "but I kept getting attacked in my sleep by some of the other men there. They were trying to take advantage of my youth and innocence, I suppose, so I left there too. I was as lost as a young man could be and had nowhere to go. I spent six months on the streets before Sister Marie took me in."

"I didn't know that's how you met Sister Marie," I said, recalling the framed picture in Peter's bedroom.

"That isn't how I originally met her, but I did live at her convent for about a year."

"How did you originally meet her?"

He didn't answer. I wasn't sure if on purpose or not.

"I thought about joining the military since I was of age at that point, and obviously I needed some discipline in my life, but I've always had this weak lung thing, asthma type stuff, and I knew that would never work. So Sister Marie started talking to me about the priesthood. Obviously she had a big influence on me going to seminary, but in a lot of ways I wound up there because I didn't know where else to go. I don't blame her for the way I feel now, all these years later. It was me who made the final decision, and to tell you the truth for a number of years it did feel like the right decision. I'd have doubts, as anyone might, but during those doubts I'd convince myself I didn't become a priest just because I had nowhere else to go. I convinced myself I had a good, specific reason for choosing this life."

"And what reason was that?"

"I wanted to make sense of suffering, my suffering, mostly. I thought if I entrenched myself in the work of God, I'd eventually find out why it all happened. A few times I thought I was close to finding an answer, but I never really did."

"Why didn't you ever tell me about this before?"

"Come on, Paul. You know me; I'm not one to open up. Besides, who on earth would want to talk about a past like that?"

I nodded. "You mentioned leaving your family and running away. Why did it come to that? How did it come to that?"

"I don't see how that's relevant."

"It's relevant because that's what started all this for you. To make peace with this you should try to understand the origins of what led you to a life on the run filled with drugs and homeless shelters. You should talk to me about this and go back even further so we can make sense of your suffering, like you said you wanted to do."

"I think I've said enough already. I don't want to relive anything else tonight."

We circled the church and navigated our way through

the garden bordering the west face. The path through the garden was narrow and forced us to walk one behind the other. Once on the back avenue behind the church we turned in the direction of our home.

"Have you told Sister Marie about this? About you wanting to leave your calling?"

"Yes, I've told her a few times actually. I think she knew I was serious this time."

"What did she say?"

"She took it in stride, like she does everything else." He suddenly laughed, surprising me considering our topic. "She calls herself the wise, old nun. She said God would bring me back when I was ready, and that if he didn't, she'd find a way to bring me back herself."

I smiled and stuffed my hands in my pockets to avoid the wind. Peter had never told me much about Sr. Marie, but it was clear how important she was to him. I knew that now more than ever. He had once told me she was a family friend, but I began to wonder if that was a lie. I wished I could contact her about Peter and what he was going through, but all I knew of Sr. Marie was that she lived in a convent somewhere down south.

"I can't really explain it, but all this kind of came to a head when I met that little girl in Costa Rica this past summer. She made me realize that I hadn't found an answer to our suffering, to mine or hers or anyone else's. When that realization hit me, I began to understand that I *did* just fall into this calling by default. I was looking for a safe roof over my head that would keep me out of trouble, and that's no reason to become a priest. I justified it back then because I was so desperate, but after a decade in the priesthood I see how out of place I actually am. I never had much faith in God to begin with. I tried to find that faith over the last ten plus years, but it's just not there. I feel like I'm living a lie. It's time I leave, Paul. That would be best for everyone, including you. I don't want you to find me passed out again like you did the other night. I'm afraid the next time you find me it might be worse than that."

"You've got it backwards, Peter. You're more likely to be found like that again if you leave. If you stay, we can keep an eye on you. You have to give this some time. You can't just steal from the Poor Box and take a midnight bus trip to the middle of nowhere."

"I have given it time."

"But you're just now telling me about it and I'm one of the people who knows you best, or at least I thought I did. Why can't you stay for a while and let me counsel you, let me help you with what you've been through. I can help you make sense of this if you'll just let me in. You're forgetting how good a priest you are. I have to help you see that so you'll realize you *are* meant for this life."

"I appreciate that, Paul, I really do. You are a good friend. But we're past that at this point. I feel like you trying to help me will only make me want to leave even more."

"A week, just give me a week to pray and think this over. You can't just leave."

We were nearing our house and walked in silence until reaching our front steps. Peter picked up his duffle bag which he'd left on the front stoop and threw it over his shoulder. I thought for a second he would take it and leave, but instead he reached back into his pocket and handed me the money.

"Will you put this back in the Poor Box tomorrow?"

"Of course."

He reached for the door and turned the knob. "Okay, Paul. I'll stay for another week."

3

OVER THE next few days in the calm of the early evenings, Walt and I fished some more. That was about the only activity we did together. But each trip down to the tide pool didn't differ much from that first day; we rarely spoke and we didn't catch much.

When I wasn't with Walt, I spent some time wandering the rest of the island, admiring the low country views and meeting the other locals, including a few old ladies down the dirt road a ways. They were kind-hearted and I enjoyed flirting with them, but I had a hard time tolerating their chit-chat. I had a better chance of stopping a hurricane coming in off the sea than I did putting an end to their long-winded stories.

I went to town and tried to eat lunch at some of the restaurants. The food was good, but I couldn't relax with the young people hopping around all about me. They spoke fast, laughed loudly, and at times it seemed they'd come from another planet. It didn't take me long to realize I should go to the market and bring my food home with me in order to keep my sanity.

At night I fixed some fine dinners: fried catfish, oysters,

shrimp n' grits, Brunswick stew, and even the simpletons like hotdogs and burgers. I read those books I had always wanted to read, the ones I'd been meaning to get to for about thirty years. I sat on my porch and looked at the stars reflecting off the Atlantic, and watched as the tides obeyed the moon.

And when the night had come and gone, I always woke up to Walt stirring the morning air with his violin.

If you knew how much I enjoyed my rest, you'd think I might hold some resentment toward him for waking me up each morning. But if you heard him play just one note on that wooden instrument, you might understand why I didn't mind so much. I heard him joke once that his fingers had begun to feel like they were stuffed full of nickels, but I swear the way he played with those stiff fingers caused the angels to stop midflight and have a listen. Each one of his notes hung in the air like the pleasant smell of a daisy. Some days I watched him from my window, enjoying the sunrise right along with his music. Other days I merely lay in bed and listened as I stared at my cracking ceiling. And still other times I would somehow find Walt's music woven into my sleep. His songs on the beach were the perfect transition from a fine dream to the beginning of a new day, though sometimes I wasn't quite sure when my dream had ended and my rising had begun.

After several invitations from Walt to go fishing, I realized I needed to return his hospitality. I decided to invite him over for dinner one evening when the summer air was just arriving. But as I went about my tiny kitchen pondering what I could prepare, I realized there was a problem: I only owned one set of dishes. Only one plate, one set of silverware, one bowl, and one cup. I liked it this way because it forced me to do the dishes after each meal. It also saved some cabinet space for books and what not.

This was going to be a problem, and could potentially be downright embarrassing. Still, I had to invite him. I moseyed on over to his back porch right before sundown, walking below tall, fluffy clouds that looked like whipped butter stacked high on top of pancakes. I climbed the rickety, wooden steps of his house for the first time and looked around. Given the small holes in the floor and the nails not hammered into the wood quite enough, I suspected Walt had built the porch himself. Two rocking chairs pointed out toward the water with a small table in between them. On top of the table rested a faded checkerboard weathered by the salty air. I immediately wondered who Walt played with; I'd never seen a soul visit him.

I heard a slight tapping coming from the other side of the porch and glanced down that way to see Sam lying on a small, dusty rug next to the screen door. He must've been tired 'cause he didn't get up, but he did give me the courtesy of wagging his tail; made a nice little rhythm as it whipped against the porch floor. I strolled over and gave him a pat on the head.

"Hey there, Sammy. You had a good, long day, have ya'?" Sam lifted his head and gave me a sniff, approving of my scent as he normally did, until a squirrel suddenly scurried by in the mulch just off the porch. Sam quickly rose and chased it up a tree, returning to my side a moment later with that sense of accomplishment dogs have after frightening off an inferior critter.

"Is that you, Buck?"

I squinted through the haziness of the screen door and saw Walt. "Yeah, it's me, neighbor."

He opened the creaky door. "What can I do for ya'?"

"Well, to repay you for taking me fishin', I thought I'd cook you dinner. You want to come on over and have a bite?" He didn't say a word. "Ole' Sammy here can come to." Sam jumped up and licked Walt's hand. We both laughed.

"Yeah," he finally said. "That sounds real nice."

"Okay, great! Why don't y'all come on over in a few; that'll give me a chance to get things goin' on the grill."

"Sounds good."

I was half way down the steps before I had to stop. "Oh, and Walt?"

"Yeah?" he replied as he reopened the screen door.

"Uh, I know this might sound strange, but can you bring over a plate a set of silverware?"

"Sure," he replied, as if I had asked him the simplest question in the world. "But I'll have to wash them first; I only got one set. I'll be over in a bit."

I chuckled before walking away.

I got my charcoal grill lit up and threw some burgers on just as Walt and Sam strolled over. He held his dishes in a plastic bag, but also carried a brown paper bag with him. "Brought you some syrup," he said. I was confused at first. No sane man puts syrup on his cheeseburger. But I understood his slang when he pulled out a bottle of Jack Daniels. "My mama always said to bring someone a gift when you come to his house for a dinner party, but that's about all I have to give. Besides, we'll put a hurtin' on it tonight."

We both laughed in agreement, although we decided to start out with a couple beers while the burgers cooked. We spoke some about our pasts, but I found myself doing most of the talking. I told him about a cross country trip I took years ago with my brother, Earl, before he passed. Walt took great interest in the story since he'd never been on such a vacation. His eyes widened when I told him about driving through the beauty of the Great Plains in Kansas and Oklahoma, and seeing the Rocky Mountains rise up in the distance before watching them fall into the Pacific in California. I also told him some about Earl and our years as auto mechanics in Gable.

I was able to learn a little about Walt's life when he told me about his service in the war, but for the most part he didn't give the impression he wanted to talk about his past. I wasn't sure if he was being polite, or he just didn't enjoy talking about himself.

We found common ground when we talked about the island: the old ladies down the dirt road, the young people, the tourists, and of course, the weather. We were old men, after all. Despite his private nature and initial gruffness, I enjoyed watching the layers fall off Walt as he got to know me. His laugh was epic, contagious in its sound and the way it made you feel as you laughed alongside him, and he was a great listener; one of those people who genuinely makes you feel like he's interested in what you're saying. This was a talent I felt that humanity underrated.

When the burgers were cooked proper we sat down on the porch steps to eat. I put some water in our two cups, laid out the condiments, and scooped some of the mac'n cheese I'd prepared on our plates. We didn't forget Sam either. He had part of a cooked patty and a bowl of water right there next to us. The sun had disappeared but it wasn't night yet. In the sky you could still see glimmers of light sprinkling the clouds as they grazed above. A gentle, summer wind blew by at all the right moments to cool us off and wisp away the mosquitoes.

After our dinner had settled, we drank a few more beers and took some swigs of Walt's syrup. It wasn't long before Walt had an idea.

"How about we go to my porch and play some checkers?"

"Yeah, I saw your board. When was the last time you played?"

"Gosh, seems like a week before never, but I suppose it's been about ten years. I sure do miss it. It's my favorite game."

"If it's your favorite game, why hadn't you played in ten years?"

"Hadn't found the right person to play with."

I smiled.

Walt, Sam and I carried the Jack Daniels to Walt's porch and settled in. To cover up some of the bitterness of the liquor, Walt went and got a small cooler and filled it with beer and ice. He had no light outside, so he lit his lantern and placed it on the floor next to our feet. Between that and the glow of the stars, we had just enough light to see the checkerboard, which sat on a wobbly, wooden table. We played two matches and split victories. We drank more beer and liquor. We got down-right drunk and laughed like goons at stupid, old-man jokes, with the moon hanging over the ocean being the only witness to our stupidity. It was a little past midnight when we started the third and final game. The mood grew tenser with each move, both of us knowing this was the championship. Then, I did something foolish, though at the time I didn't know it would be so foolish.

I asked Walt a question.

It was a simple question, one I thought was harmless. But I suppose my drunken state caused me to think it was more harmless than it actually was.

"Say, Walt," I said after making a move, "why is it you go out on the beach in the mornin' and play that violin a' yours?" Walt didn't flinch. He stared down at the board intently, as if his next move would decide the fate of his life. After he had made his move, I repeated my question. "Why do you play your violin in the mornings, Walt?" Again he ignored me. I made a quick move without thinking. "You gunna answer my question, Walt? I know ya' hear me." He quickly capitalized on my bad move and took one of my men. He placed the chip on top of my other fallen chips and looked to me with eyes I had not yet seen from him.

"You ain't quite there yet, Buck."

I made another foolish move.

"What does that mean? It's only a simple question."

"Are you going to take this game seriously? That's the second boneheaded move you've made in a row." Walt jumped my man and landed on the last row of squares. "Now king me."

I placed a chip atop the one that had landed on my back row, giving him a tall and mobile king. But I didn't much care about the game anymore. "I'll be able to concentrate on the game if you at least give me a reason for why you don't want to answer my question."

"Time just ain't right yet. All good things in time."

I puffed my chest, making another quick move in the game. This time it wasn't a bad one. Walt settled back in to the game and pondered his next move. But I couldn't let go of our other topic. "I'm sorry, but I just don't see—"

"Drop it or the game's over."

I nearly swallowed my tongue when he snapped at me. I decided to call his bluff. "Maybe the game *should* be over then."

Walt stood up, grabbed his cup of whisky and headed for his screen door. "Come on, Sam," he said as he opened the door. The frightened dog knew Walt meant business as he scurried into the house with his tail between his legs. I sat there alone on Walter Henderson's back porch, with nothing but a checkerboard and lantern to keep me company. I didn't move for about ten minutes, thinking Walt would come back outside at some point. But he never did.

I stumbled back home and climbed into bed. I couldn't imagine why my question had sparked such a tense response from Walt. But as I continued to think about it, I eventually passed out.

A few hours later, I awoke to the sound of Walt playing his violin.

4

MY CONVERSATION with Peter weighed on me over the next twenty-four hours. I slept with a sensitive ear, wondering if I would hear our front door open and close again, signaling Peter's departure from my life forever. When I *was* able to fall asleep, I experienced a nightmare. I saw that little girl from Costa Rica who Peter had told me about. She walked out of a village set ablaze with fire, slowly approaching me as other panicked villagers ran wildly in the background. The scene was chaotic, but I could hear her clearly as she whispered into my ear the same question Peter had asked. *"How does God let this happen?"* I'd wake up in a hot flash before I could answer with sweat drenching my body. Each time this happened I was disappointed; I wondered what answer my subconscious self would give to such a question.

I prayed for guidance on how to reach Peter but found no answers. He went about his daily duties just as he had done for the last several years, but he barely spoke a word and behaved like a zombie. I knew at any point I could return to our home and his belongings would be gone.

Three days after the night he nearly left, an unexpected

envelope appeared underneath our office door. We were both working at our desks when it came flying into the room. We looked at each other.

"I'll do the honors," I said as I rose from my desk.

"Take a look out the door," Peter suggested.

I picked up the envelope and opened our door. The school hallway was empty and dark, with only a thin layer of dust on the tile floor and a light flickering with fragile life from the ceiling. "No one out there," I informed him. I opened the white envelope and read the letter folded up inside. "It says we're supposed to go see Father Chase in the morning—at six, before we go to breakfast."

"Concerning what?"

"Doesn't say."

I handed Peter the letter and leaned up against my desk.

"That's strange," he said after confirming what I had read.

I lay in bed that night trying to think of what our upcoming meeting could be about. I wondered if it had to do with what Peter and I had spoken about last week, but I didn't think he had said anything to anyone else, and surely I wouldn't be involved in such a meeting.

The Most Reverend Father Charles Huckle, known to most as Father Chase, was the president of the college. But despite his position, he was more like a father to me and Peter, rather than our boss. Anytime he wanted to see us we usually spoke in passing, or he told us to come by his office later that day. This secretive letter, informing us to tell no one about the meeting, was more than unusual.

The next morning, we woke early, while darkness still blanketed the campus. A burst of chilly air struck us as we opened the front door of our house. The grounds were empty since most of the students with early classes didn't go to breakfast until seven.

When we made it to the rectory hall where Father Chase's office was, we saw that his secretary was not yet in, but his office light flooded the outside waiting room. We also heard music. A peaceful symphony flowed through his door and into the lobby, music we associated with our college president and told us he was already in his office. We glanced through the doorway and saw Father Chase sitting behind his desk in his faded, lavender chair, appearing like he may have been sleeping.

"Father Chase?" Peter said with a slight knock on the door, trying his best not to disturb him.

The elderly priest opened his eyes.

"Come on in, you two." He reached across the mahogany desk and turned off his stereo. "Were you waiting long?"

"Oh, no," Peter replied. "We just walked in."

"Please, sit down."

Peter and I took our places in the two wooden seats sitting opposite his desk. A large crucifix hung on the wall behind him, while the two side walls were lined with books. A small cot sat in the back corner of the office resting under a painting of a guardian angel. The cot was not normally there; I wondered how busy Father Chase had been these last few days.

"How are you two doing?"

I glanced at Peter. "We're fine," he answered for the both of us. I nodded in agreement, knowing for sure now that Peter had not mentioned his intention of leaving the priesthood to anyone other than me. It also let me know that I clearly had no idea what this meeting was about.

"Well," Father Chase began, "I won't waste anyone's time. It's early and I don't want you to miss breakfast. Something has come up, and the Bishop has a request for us, or rather, a Bishop from a neighboring diocese has requested our help."

"Are we being transferred?" I interrupted.

"No, no. This matter will probably be a short one. Perhaps only a day or two." His words trailed off at the end of his sentences, as if he was unsure of how to finish them.

"What is it then?" Peter asked.

"There has been a supposed apparition of sorts, involving a statue of the Virgin Mary, at a church in Jamestown, Rhode Island."

"What sort of happening?" I asked.

"Where is Jamestown?" Peter added.

He sat up and folded his hands. "Jamestown is a very small, harbor town located on Conanicut Island. It's just outside Newport and south of Providence. From what I hear it has a quaint downtown area that hosts tourists from time-to-time, but the Catholic Church is further out in a remote area, sitting on the cliffs overlooking Mackerel Cove. It's called Our Lady of the Sea, a very small parish with only a couple hundred parishioners. Have either of you ever been to Rhode Island?"

Both of us shook our heads.

"So what has happened with this statue?" Peter asked.

"Well, first let me tell you something that I'm sure you already know. The Church is very careful about how they handle these situations. There are a lot of people in the world and not all can be trusted. It's unfortunate to have to say this, but the Vatican very rarely recognizes these types of events. They have to be careful in how they handle these claims, following a strict set of rules at all times. They can't just accept every supposed miracle on a whim, as much as we would want those miracles to be true."

"Of course," I said. "We teach a section in our classes about Marian apparitions. We know all about the procedures the Church takes."

"I know you do, and that's part of the reason you've been chosen for this. You weren't the first choice, mind you, but I'll get into that in a bit."

"Father," Peter said with a crack in his voice, "you still haven't told us what has happened with the statue."

Father Chase took a heavy breath. "It's giving off heat."

"What?" I asked.

"How much heat?" Peter added.

"Good question. A statue giving off heat is strange enough, but it's the amount of heat that has people worried. At first it was only a slight warmth, apparently like standing near a heat vent in your house. The local priest ignored it; said he thought it was his imagination. But as the days went on the statue got hotter and hotter. At this point, they say entering the church feels like walking into an oven."

"Are they sure the statue is the source of the heat?" Peter asked.

"Well as I mentioned, the local priest said he felt the statue getting warmer in the days leading up to all this. But also, there's a parishioner there who's a part of the local fire department. He went inside the church with some kind of gadget, and his little meters and scales apparently went haywire when he approached it."

"Of course I find this amazing," I said, "but what are *we*

supposed to do? And what did you say about us not being the first choice?"

"I was getting to that. You see, an odd chain of events has led to this meeting. The local priest in Jamestown called the Bishop of Rhode Island when all this started happening. The Bishop there is a good friend of our Bishop Robert in Boston, and after much discussion the two of them decided they would contact Father Timothy Wilson to do an investigation, because of his expertise on such matters. I know you both know Father Timothy, especially you, Paul."

"Yes, of course," I said, thinking back on my old teacher from seminary. Father Timothy may not have been known to the general public, but in Catholic circles he was a renowned and well respected scholar who had spent many years studying and teaching Church practices. He was the author of several books, including a best seller written about the most famous Marian apparitions of the past few centuries. I had developed a close friendship with him after my years studying under him. That friendship had opened up doors for me in the past, and apparently was continuing to do so today.

"Unfortunately, Father Timothy has fallen ill," Father Chase went on. "We don't think it's anything serious, but he cannot make the journey from New York to Rhode Island. After hearing about this supposed happening, he recommended that you be contacted, Paul, to go in his stead and conduct an investigation. Your former teacher thinks very highly of you and has plenty of confidence that you'll be able to do what we ask."

Peter fidgeted in his seat next to me.

"But I don't want Paul going alone on this. I know you

two are friends and work well together, so I'd like you to go with him, Peter." Peter nodded but avoided eye contact with both me and Father Chase. "Now, all we want from you is to determine the validity of the claim. The Church will not waste time on this if it turns out to be a hoax of some kind, which it very well could be. The small-town community is terrified by this and the local priest is overwhelmed, so when you get there, assure the people you're doing what you can to make sense of it all. But mostly, get yourself in front of that statue and report back to me about it. Of course if the opportunity presents itself, ask questions and speak with the parishioners. Even though this is only a preliminary examination, I want to be able to tell the Bishops as much as we can. After we've done our part, they'll decide if Cardinal Hargrove should be contacted, and it will then be *his* decision on whether or not to get the Vatican involved. I hope you don't get down there and discover the statue is perfectly normal and the parish has gone mad, or that this is all a big hoax, but you never know."

Peter and I didn't speak for a few seconds as we let everything sink in.

"I wouldn't agree to send you down there if I didn't feel this deserved our attention. I myself would love to go, and I'm sure both the Bishops would love to check it out for themselves, but we have too many pressing matters that demand our attention. If you get down there and find this to be of the utmost importance for the Church, I'm sure we'll all be taking a visit to this little harbor town eventually. Is this something you think you can handle?"

"Of course," I said. "When do we leave?"

"We want you on the Boston Commuter Rail which can

get you to the train station in time to catch the nine o'clock to Providence. Once there, someone will pick you up and drive you to Jamestown, one of the local parishioners, I think."

"Why have we not heard about this on CNN or something?" Peter asked.

"Ah, yes, well, there are a few reasons for that, I suppose. For one, this has only been going on for about a week, but as I said, Jamestown is a very small town. I know there are good people there but they tend to keep to themselves. I don't think they would care much for national reporters invading their quaint town, so they may be choosing to keep quiet on their own. But I also don't think many people outside the Catholic parish know about it yet. The Bishop of Rhode Island advised the local priest to keep his people quiet until we do an investigation, an investigation that doesn't get tainted or distracted by the news media. Now you know why I was so secretive about our meeting, with my letter and all. I would've just popped in your office last night to meet with you but I had a previous obligation, so I got a student employee to drop off the letter. And speaking of your students, I'll have to tell them you're on a mission assignment for a few days and we'll get you some substitutes."

We shook hands with Father Chase and thanked him again for the opportunity. It took us about thirty minutes to eat a quick breakfast and get back to our house where we packed a small bag. I rambled all the way to the commuter rail station, asking countless questions, most of which Peter ignored. I could tell I was annoying him but I couldn't contain my enthusiasm. In all my studies, I couldn't recall a statue of Mary giving off heat. I had heard about tears of blood streaming from the eyes of statues, I had read about statues giving off the smell of roses, and I remembered stories of statues falling over for no apparent reason, but never anything like what we were journeying to witness today.

We boarded the commuter rail that would carry us over the suburban neighborhoods and deliver us into Boston in a half hour. Once seated, I decided to take advantage of this opportunity where Peter could not get away from me.

"Are you still going to leave?"

"I'm not sure," he answered without looking at me. He reached out and rubbed a piece of fuzz off the seat in front of us. "I'd be lying if I said I wasn't intrigued by this supposed phenomenon, but that doesn't mean anything has changed from how I felt last week. This heated statue won't change anything in my life. You heard Father Chase; I wasn't even supposed to be making this trip. I'm just coming to keep you company, to be your chaperone. I'll do this out of respect for Father Chase. After that, I'll try and make a concrete decision about my future."

5

WHEN I went to bed after our argument, I felt that Walt had behaved like a jerk, and there was no other way to say it. But when I awoke the next day and replayed the hazy memory, I realized I was probably overstepping my boundaries with a little help from the alcohol. A sober Buck Washington would've dropped the issue when it was clear Walt didn't want to discuss his morning ritual.

Still, I was a stubborn old man, and I wasn't going to apologize. I saw Walt coming and going from his house and he saw me, but other than a few stolen glances there wasn't much communication between us. Even Sam was ignoring me, which I didn't know dogs could do. I began to wonder if Walt and I would ever speak again.

I woke up late one Sunday morning about ten o'clock. I was eating a bowl of cereal on my back porch when I heard Walt's pickup truck pull in on the front side of his house. I knew he was returning from church. He went every Sunday to the early service at the local Catholic church, where he had been head of the choir for many years. His devotion to church attendance always found a way to make me feel guilty. I had been meaning to find the local AME Church every week since I'd moved to Edisto, but it was no real surprise that I hadn't got around to it yet. I kept telling myself I would do it the following Monday. When Monday came, I said I'd do it Tuesday, and so on and so forth. But I never took note of my procrastination until I saw Walt come home from his own service each Sunday.

Just as I finished scooping up the last soggy flakes of my cereal, I heard the slam of my neighbor's screen door. I looked over and saw Walt holding his fishing poles and tackle box. I pretended I didn't notice him. But not a minute later I heard a familiar question.

"Want to go fishin'?"

I turned around and there stood Walt and Sam.

"Sure."

We walked down the beach, this time to a public dock stretching out into the creek side of the island. It went about fifty yards into the water, past the saw grass and muddy sand dwellings of the hermit crabs. We sat on the edge of the dock and cast our lines as the smell of saltwater and plough mud mixed together, giving off that unique, low country aroma I'd grown accustomed to liking even though it wasn't the most pleasing smell. I was amazed at how we could act as if nothing had happened. It didn't take long for us to get engrossed in a sports conversation. I had truly forgotten about our heated moment from the week before, but suddenly, Walt interrupted me.

"I'm sorry I was so rude the other night."

He'd caught me off guard, but I replied, "No, no. I was at fault."

"I think maybe we both were a little. But I overreacted."

I waited to see if he wanted to say more, but I continued when he seemed to be finished. "I shouldn't have pried like that."

"Well, you asked a pretty fair question. It's not normal for a grown man to play the violin on the beach each morning." I didn't know what to say back to that. It wasn't normal. "I'm just a private man, Buck. It took a lot for me to come over and ask you to go fishing that one day, but I felt I should since you were the first person to move into that house in years. I felt like that was the neighborly thing to do, and I'm glad I did 'cause you're probably the closest thing I've had to a friend in the last ten years."

"I'm like that myself. I want to be alone most of the time, but I enjoy you and Sam's company. I'm glad you came over."

Sam perked his head up at hearing his name, but quickly returned to his midday nap. He was in no mood to listen to this conversation between old men.

Walt sighed. "I play for my wife."

"Your wife?"

"She's passed on."

"Oh, gosh, I'm sorry, Walt." He looked out over the wandering see for nearly a minute without saying anything. I wondered if that was the end of this. "You want to talk about it anymore?"

He rubbed at the scruff on his face.

"She grew up in my hometown, friends since childhood. Our families lived down the street from one another, with only two houses separating us. You could argue we were together since the first day we met, runnin' around as little kids and getting into trouble, but we didn't officially start dating until high school."

"High school sweethearts, huh?"

He nodded. "Our story was a typical, American romance— she was the head cheerleader and I was the star quarterback, with everything and anything you could ever ask for. After high school real life set in a little, like it always does, but we were still happy. We both got jobs; I worked on a dairy farm and she started working as a part-time nurse. We were set to get married when I got drafted for the war; almost rushed through a ceremony, but decided to wait. Thankfully, I survived my time overseas and we were married when I got back."

"What was her name?"

"Olivia. Olivia Wade Henderson."

"Tell me more about her. What'd she look like?"

Walt closed his eyes briefly, as if he were trying to find her behind his eyelids.

"Her hair was long and dark," he finally said, reopening his eyes, "almost down to her waist and perfectly straight. She was real tiny, only five-foot, two-inches, and not much more'n a hundred pounds. But it was her eyes that everyone loved about her. They were a light hazel color and as deep as the ocean. Of course I'm biased in saying she was pretty, but you'll have to trust me when I say everyone loved her eyes."

"Maybe you could show me a picture of her when we get back."

"Why wait?" Walt leaned to his side and pulled a picture from his wallet. His description of Olivia had been spot on.

"You weren't lying about those eyes," I agreed.

I returned the picture to him and he placed it back in

his wallet. "She's been gone almost thirty-five years now, but every day feels like I just lost her the day before."

After a short pause, I said, "So, you play for *her* when you're out on the beach?"

"My mother passed away shortly after Olivia and I were married. Mom left me her old violin, the one she'd taught me lessons on when I was younger. I surprisingly had a knack for it, and Olivia loved to hear me play. I bought some music books at the local store and did some practicing. I played every morning for her before we went to work; got better with each passing month. My favorite part of playing was watching her face as she listened to my songs. That's the face I see when I go out there each morning."

"You've been doing this for over thirty years?" He nodded. "You sure you ain't missed one day in all those years?"

"Never."

"That sure does take some kind a' dedication."

"If you knew her, you'd know why I do it."

"I've never been that way with a woman. Then again, I don't know if I could get one to be that devoted to me."

We fished in silence for a few minutes.

"Did you and Olivia live here in Edisto?"

"No, we lived in Aiken over by the Georgia border, where we grew up. I moved here a few months after she died. I planned on it being temporary; just wanted to get away for a while and clear my head. But one day I decided to go out on the beach for an early walk. I saw the sun coming up, warming the water and dabbing the sky, and knew I had to play. I ran and got my violin and I've lived here ever since. For some reason, being close to the water makes me feel closer to her."

"That makes sense," I replied. At first I thought I was just being polite, but that really did make sense. Heaven always seemed to be just on the other side of an oceanic horizon. Sometimes I wish I were a better swimmer.

Just then I felt a tug on my line. I stood up and began to reel it in. Walt stood up too and encouraged me.

"Come on, man!" he yelled. "Bring that sucker in! I know you're stronger than that!"

The moment was a perfect break from the somber feel that had come over us. After about three minutes, I had lifted a sizable, ten-pound trout out of the sea. That might not be big to some, but for my old bones it was quite a catch. We threw it in our cooler and headed back home. As we walked down the beach, the seagulls swirled above us, hoping we'd leave them a meal on the sand.

The day had reached the point where a nap would be real suitable. I couldn't wait to go inside, throw the fish in the freezer and throw myself into bed. I told Walt to come over in a couple hours so he could help me prepare our dinner and listen to some jazz music I'd wanted him to hear.

"So you don't mind, right?" Walt asked before we went into our separate homes.

"Mind what?"

"Me playing in the morning."

"Are you kiddin'? Your violin is the best alarm clock a man could have."

"I don't want to wake you up; maybe I'll start going farther down the beach. No one has lived in that house for years so I never considered how you could hear me."

"I enjoy hearing you play each morning, Walt. Besides, I

can fall back asleep as easy as baby." I held out my hand. "All right?"

"Sure," he replied, accepting the handshake. We began to walk away from each other, but Walt called me back. "Oh, and Buck." He jogged over to me. "Thought you might want this based on somethin' you said the other day."

He reached into his pocket and handed me a folded-up sheet of paper. Before I could open it he turned around and returned to his house. I placed the cooler on the ground and unfolded the paper.

I smiled when I read it:

St. James AME Church
202 W. Atlantic St.
Edisto Island, SC 29438

6

AFTER OUR ride into Providence, we stepped off the train and entered the station, not knowing who would be waiting for us. But it wasn't long before we spotted a middle-aged woman with pale, snow-white skin shouting our names.

"Father Paul! Father Peter! Is that you? Oh, of course it's you. Two traveling priests aren't common in this train station." She scurried up to us and shook our hands. "My name is Juliet O'Day. It's so nice to meet you."

She was a small lady, dressed very plainly, like she may have been a librarian, in flat brown shoes, an ankle-length, brown wool dress and a white blouse that fluffed up to her chin and hung beyond her wrists.

After our greetings, she took my arm and said, "Come on out this way. I'm parked over here."

We followed Mrs. O'Day into the asphalt parking lot as she went on about the cold weather they'd been having this week. It was rather chilly out, but no different than the fall weather we were used to in Massachusetts. Eventually she stopped in front of a two-door car that appeared more like a go-cart, royal blue and not much longer than my wingspan. "Good thing you boys don't own much, huh?" she joked.

Peter and I threw our bags in the miniature trunk and had a staring contest to determine who would have to sit in the back. I lost. I climbed in first and compressed my body crossways in the back seat.

We left the train station in Providence and went south on a highway curving between green hills and grassy pastures. Off both sides of the road, rundown barns dotted the landscape, along with the occasional windmill spinning its sails in the wind. The leaves of the trees were in the midst of their autumn transformation, blending together to form the picturesque hollows of the New England countryside.

As she drove, Mrs. O'Day gave us a history about her state, at times more concerned with her dialog then her driving, which made me nervous enough to recite a prayer. When her lesson hit a lull, I waited to see if Peter would bring up the reason why we were there, but he didn't, so I did.

"So Mrs. O'Day," I said from the back seat, "what can you tell us about this statue?"

"Oh, yes," she said with a sigh, "*the* statue. It has brought so much fear and controversy to our little parish. No one knows what's happening, but people all have their opinions. Some claim we simply have a busted heat system, others claim it's a sign of the apocalypse. I'm so glad you two were able to come down to straighten this all out."

"Please don't think we'll have a quick answer for you," I said. "There's no handbook to refer to on these things."

"But you two are experts, right?"

Peter glanced over his shoulder at me. "We've both spent

time studying these types of things," he answered her. "But just as Father Paul said, there's never a clear answer for why these things happen. Now what can you tell us about all this?" Peter took out a pad and paper.

"What do you want to know?"

"When did the statue first start to give off heat? Who noticed it? When was the last time *you* stood before the statue?"

"Well, I believe it was Father Powell who first noticed the heat."

"Your local priest?" Peter asked.

"Yes, he's been with us about five years, I think. It was just before the Sunday Mass at nine-thirty, almost two weeks ago. Father Powell made a joke about it in his homily. He said he thought he had noticed our statue of the Virgin Mother giving off heat before everyone arrived for Mass. He said she must be trying to warm us up before the really cold weather arrives. We can sometimes get the coldest winters here. Have either of you ever been to Rhode Island before?"

"So about two weeks ago, you said?" Peter asked as he jotted things down in his notebook.

"Oh, yes, I'm sorry. After Mass, some of us approached the statue out of curiosity. I thought I felt a little warmth coming from it, but others disagreed and said it was only Father Powell's imagination. No one thought much of it at first."

"Where is the statue located in the church?" I asked.

"Why does that matter?"

"It probably doesn't. We're just trying to get all the information we can."

"It's at the front of the church," she replied returning her eyes to the road, "on the left side of the altar, in a little alcove of sorts."

"So after that first Sunday," Peter said, "how long was it before people started to *really* take notice of the heat?"

"Like I said, you should talk to Father Powell."

"We will," I assured her, "but we want to hear from more than just him."

She scrunched her face as she searched her memory. "I remember Molly Dinkins mentioning something to me first. She's an older friend of mine who goes to daily Mass just about every day. Deaf as a doorknob, but never met a better Bridge player in all my life."

I steered her back to topic. "And what did Ms. Dinkins say?"

"Oh, something about it getting hotter. I usually go with her to daily Mass, but I was very busy that day. I didn't really believe Molly until I went to Mass the next Sunday. I heard people murmuring about it in the narthex. Some said it was too hot to go inside, while others said it wasn't so bad and people were just overreacting. But I went in, convinced not to miss my Sunday obligation. And boys, I will tell you, it was hotter than fire in there. Some parishioners didn't make it through the first reading. By the end of Mass, there weren't but ten people in the church. But things didn't get really scary until this week. I showed up for daily Mass on Tuesday, and Father Powell was standing out front looking horrified. He had locked the doors of the church and said it was too hot for anyone to enter. He said it was dangerous." She turned to Peter with wide eyes, startled with the memory. "Do you know how strange that sounds? To have your priest tell you it's too dangerous to enter your own church?"

"I can't imagine how that made you feel," Peter said as he continued to write down things in his notepad.

"Anyway," she went on, "Father Powell held a meeting at a parishioner's house that night. He told us he would contact the Bishop and see how to handle this, but to not speak of the statue around town until we could figure out what was going on. I've been tempted to tell my friends who don't go to our church, but I'm too afraid to talk about it. I feel like I might get in trouble, or worse, upset God in some way. Who knows? Maybe he already is upset with us. It's just been a very frightening couple of weeks, Fathers. I lost my husband recently and without him here this has been even more difficult."

"I'm sorry for your loss," I offered from the backseat. "How did he die?"

"Cancer." She glanced down at her wedding ring and rubbed it with her opposite hand.

"We'll be sure to keep you and him in our prayers," I said. "I'm sorry you've had to go through all this after losing him."

"Oh, thank you, Father. One can never have too many prayers said for them."

We rode in silence for the next several minutes as the sound of the rolling tires filled our ears, until soon we exited onto an off ramp.

"Where are you taking us first?" Peter asked.

"I'm supposed to take you to my home so you can drop off your belongings and freshen up. When you're ready, I'll take you to the church where you can meet Father Powell and the firemen."

"Firemen?" Peter said.

"The head of our fire department goes to Our Lady of the Sea. He and one of his men have been helping Father Powell. And it's a good thing, too; it's not safe to enter without the right people."

Peter glanced back at me with a raise of his brow.

We made our way over a steel bridge stretching above the harbor. Below us, the water churned in choppy waves cloaked in a dark, green tint. Several sailboats bounced further out in the sea before a white and black lighthouse. Its gleaming light spun in circles, warning of the rocky island it stood upon and only visible during midday because of the cloud cover darkening the land.

Across the bridge, we arrived in the quaint town of Jamestown. We circled around a port of docked boats and into the main part of town. It had a village feel to it despite being modern at the same time. Shops full of trinkets lined the streets, along with old Victorian-style inns and plenty of restaurants to appease the tourists. Once through the town we moved into a string of neighborhoods bordered by red maples and sidewalks, eventually arriving at Mrs. O'Day's house just before noon. It was a small, brick home with white shutters and a white picket fence to match. We parked in the narrow driveway and made our way inside her snug and cozy home. Pictures from her past adorned the walls and handmade quilts draped outdated furniture. She gave us a brief tour of the house, taking pride in the beautiful view from her back deck which rested over a forest turned red and yellow by the autumn chill. She eventually showed us to our bedrooms which sat perched at the top of the stairs, separated by a bathroom.

After a thirty minute break to get off our feet and eat lunch, our investigation awaited. We left Mrs. O'Day's neighborhood and went back through the main part of town. Our timid nerves quieted our tongues, leaving only the chamber music playing on her radio.

The town streets and neighborhoods gave way to a rural area after only a few minutes. Farmland where sheep and cows grazed stretched over the horizon. We rounded a bend in the road curving around a small but thick forest and came upon a hill; at the top of that hill rested an old, stone church. I immediately knew this parish must have lacked the proper funds to have a Rec Hall or a house built nearby for the local priest, as the church sat alone on the hill.

A few cars and a red SUV with the fire department logo on the side were parked in the gravel parking lot out front. Several figures stood waiting on the church's steps, one dressed in black from head to toe, an outfit I was familiar with. As we continued our way up the road, I noticed that Our Lady of the Sea overlooked a cliff dropping down into the bay. A well-tended flower garden along the left of the church brought charm to the small structure, and exquisite stained glass windows ran from the roof almost down to the ground interrupting the stone pattern of the outside walls.

"That's Father Powell up there," Mrs. O'Day said as we pulled in. "He will welcome you. Take as long as you need; you're in his hands now. And here's a key to my home in case I'm out or you get back too late. I probably won't be out, though, I don't know of any late-night functions going on for fifty-year-old women."

Mrs. O'Day handed me the key as she chuckled at her

own joke. Her humor seemed like a forced attempt to disguise her discomfort from returning to the church grounds. We had barely stepped out of the tiny, blue car before she peeled out of the parking lot.

Father Powell waved to us from the front steps and came our way.

"Father Paul, Father Peter, I presume," he said as he approached us. "Thank you for coming."

"Absolutely," I said, shaking his hand. His balding, grey hair showed his age, as did the bags under his eyes, and his skin drooped off his face like worn leather on a baseball mitt. We exchanged pleasantries with him, listening to the exhaustion in his voice.

"Well, I know we don't have you for much time," Father Powell said, breaking us away from our greetings. "What else would you like to know before you go inside?"

"I'm curious about what day the statue began to give off heat," I began. "Throughout history, there have been Marian miracles involving statues that occurred on the anniversary of important dates."

"Yes, I thought about that. I can't say for sure the exact day, because the small amount of heat the statue was giving off at first may have gone unnoticed. But the first time I became aware was Sunday, the fifth."

Peter opened a small book from his satchel and flipped through the pages. "September fifth doesn't sound like any type of feast day for the Virgin Mother, and off the top of my head I don't know of any other Marian apparitions on that day." After Peter found the correct day, he continued. "The fifth is the feast day of St. Laurence Justinian, the first Patri-arch of Venice."

The three of us searched for any connection we could make.

"Do you have any parishioners with an Italian heritage?" I asked, knowing I was reaching. "Maybe one who has been sick?"

"No, not at all."

"Does the church itself have Italian roots?" I asked.

Father Powell shook his head. "This church was built about thirty-five years ago by the Catholics of Jamestown. They were tired of driving to Newport for Mass, so they raised the money with the help of the diocese. They wanted their own identity here on the island, but there's nothing really spe-cial to take note of with that."

"Actually, I'm not sure we can place any significance on the date," Peter interjected. "A lot of times when a statue does something like this, there's a clear moment for its beginning. It's hard to miss tears of blood or something along those lines. But with this there's too much obscurity. When did it become so hot that you couldn't enter the church?"

"Shortly after the next Sunday, on the fourteenth, I think. I tried to pray at the foot of the statue, but it was just too hot. I called some people I know at the local fire department, not knowing who else to contact. Those two men over there, actually," he said pointing toward them. "They did a scan of the area and didn't find anything out of the ordinary. When people showed up for Mass that day, I couldn't let them in. I canceled all the daily Masses, and shortly after that, I called the Bishop, and here you two are."

"We were surprised that we hadn't heard about this on the news, yet," I said. "How have you avoided that?"

"Things are a little different here than they are in the big city. Most people in this town, in this parish, I should say, understand that the national media would overrun us if word got out about the statue, and they don't want that. I advised them to keep quiet, but honestly, I don't think people want to talk about it. Some residents feel the Virgin Mary is trying to warn us of God's impending wrath, like we have angered him somehow. My parishioners are too scared to leave their homes right now."

"I think we should go ahead and get in there and save our other questions for afterwards," I offered.

"Okay, sure."

"Is there anything else we should know?" Peter asked him.

He hesitated. "Let me go speak with the men who'll be taking you inside before I introduce you to them."

We followed him up toward the red SUV parked in front of the church, but allowed him to go speak with the other two men in private as we looked out over the Atlantic. The seawater rumbled angrily below us, crashing against the towering cliffs sprawled up and down the coastline. The cliffs were rocky and rigid and covered in a green moss that shined in the light of day. A trio of pelicans gliding inches above the waterline caught my eye, but just then a deep voice boomed from behind us. "So you're the guys we're taking inside, huh?"

We turned around, met by two men, one large and towering with a scruffy beard, the other a younger man with a chiseled, youthful face. They wore thick, black suits they weren't wearing a moment ago, seemingly made from rubber.

It went up to their necks and extended down into their boots and gloves, both made from the same material. No part of their skin was visible except for their neck and face.

"I'm Sergeant Roger Hampton," the large, bearded one said, "and this is Burt Chavis." Sergeant Hampton had a rigid manner and stiff face. Burt, younger and more timid, had a jittery handshake. I wondered if he was frightened because of the statue, but knew Sergeant Hampton was the type of man who wouldn't show his fear even if he felt it.

"Will we be wearing something like this as well?" Peter asked.

"Yeah, we've got two suits ready for you. It's a little over two hundred degrees in there. You could stay in there for a minute or two without the suits, but they'll help with your breathing and allow us to stay in there longer than we would without them. Otherwise you'd probably pass out after too long. Unless you think your priest outfits will protect you, that is."

"I think we'll take the suits," I answered him.

He motioned for Burt to help us into the awkward getups and walked back toward the church. After helping us, Burt fell back as well and stood behind his boss, leaving us alone with Father Powell as we made some last minute adjustments to our gloves and boots.

"Mrs. O'Day said these firemen were members of the parish," I said.

"They are," Father Powell answered.

"Then why does it seem like the Sergeant despises us?"

"Don't take that personally. He's been through a rough couple of years. He and his wife lost a child recently and he hasn't been coming to church since. The Sergeant has always been a little rough around the edges, but I reached out to him because of his expertise and because I felt he could keep quiet about what was going on. Perhaps he resents being here, but his wife is still an active member of the parish, so I suppose he still feels a sense of obligation to us for that reason. I owe him a great deal of gratitude for what he's done in the last few days."

I glanced at the Sergeant, viewing him differently now than I did moments ago. It reminded me to never judge someone. I couldn't say that my faith wouldn't also be stolen if I had buried a child.

Father Powell escorted us over towards the church as we waddled in our suits. "Are you coming in there with us?" Peter asked.

"No. I know how hot it is in there."

Our conversation ended when we arrived at the church steps where the two firemen waited. They held large, rounded masks in their hands which I figured would go on our heads.

"Now, when we get inside," Sergeant Hampton began, "you two have to listen to me. If I feel like something isn't right and we need to leave at the drop of a hat, we will leave. It's hotter than hell in there and I don't feel good about what's going on inside this church. For all I know this place could go up in flames any minute. I may not have figured this out just yet, but I sure as heck don't see how you two are going to help."

"You're in control," I assured him.

We pulled the headpiece and shield onto our heads and snapped the dangling flaps into place on our shoulders, chest and back. The sound of my own breathing echoed inside my mask, clouding my thoughts just as much as it clouded the glass face of the mask. We journeyed up the seven church steps behind Sergeant Hampton and Burt, each step made slowly and with great care.

Sergeant Hampton opened the red, oak doors and led us into the narthex. Once inside, I glanced back and saw Father Powell watching us with a face of stone.

The doors shut and he was gone.

I turned around and was engulfed by a wave of heat. It was hotter than anything I'd ever felt or could have imagined. I wanted to be inside this church from the moment Father Chase had told us about the infamous heated statue of our Virgin Mother, now I only wanted to leave this place and never return.

7

AFTER WALT gave me the address to the St. James AME Church, I went the very next Sunday. The minister seemed to be a good man, and the people I met after the service were all as friendly as they could be. As I drove back home, I felt real fine about myself, like sitting in that church pew for just over an hour changed my outlook on things, like suddenly all my sins had been forgiven and I would never sin again. Course an hour later I got to lying to the old ladies down the road about why I couldn't come in and have tea with them. Instead, I took a walk.

As I strolled around the lonely streets of the island, my thoughts kept returning to Walt. I still listened to him play his violin each morning, but I listened with a different ear now that I knew the reasons behind why he played. I admired him for his dedication and the love he had for a woman he hadn't seen in thirty-five years.

Thirty-five years.

I thought about that number a lot. Walt was probably in his seventies, maybe late sixties, and he said they'd married in their early twenties. By my math, which was never very good, they couldn't have been married for long. Even after the story he told me I pictured Olivia to be an older woman who had just left this world. But in reality, she must've been a young girl when she passed, not much older than the picture he'd shown me in his wallet. I wouldn't dare pry into the reasons behind her death, though. I had learned my lesson from before. Walt was a private man. If he wanted me to know something, he would tell me in his own time.

For the next year the two of us fell into a nice rhythm, something men of our age treasure. We fished together, played checkers, and took walks around the shore bend of the island. We journeyed to a nearby mall just before Christmas of 1989 and bought each other a special present—an extra dish set. That solved what seemed to be our biggest problem and made our dinners together more convenient. During that holiday time I drove us up to Gable so I could introduce him to my nephew. Earl's only son was a good, young man with a wife and child. I took pride in introducing Walt to my kin. By the time we left their home two days later, I realized I was also proud to introduce them to Walt.

Olivia stayed close to my thoughts, especially each morning when I heard Walt play. But no matter how much my curiosity ate at me, I never asked about her death, nor did he ever tell me. It was as though Walt was testing my patience as a friend. In order to get a glimpse into that part of his life, I had to further earn his trust. I suppose I finally earned that trust one August day in 1990.

We had fished countless times off the nearby docks and sandy beaches, but a young restaurant owner in town named Connor Sullivan had become one of my good friends and offered to take us out on his boat. He said he'd seen Walt and me fishing off the docks many times and wanted to give us the chance to go out to sea. Connor had a boat he claimed was nothing special, but it sure was something special to a couple old men who had never fished offshore.

He took us out real early in the morning, before the sun had greeted the sky. In fact, it was so early Walt had to perform his morning ritual in the black tint of the pre-dawn hours. He later told me it was the first time he'd played on the beach with the stars still hanging above him.

Once the three of us got out on the water, we stayed there for nearly five hours. It was a strange feeling to be out so far that the land disappeared into the morning haze. Somehow I felt that all my problems had been left anchored on the sand back home. The open sea acted as a kind of refuge, cleansing my weathered soul of its many blemishes. As we floated several miles offshore, we caught fish that doubled the size of the ones we had caught off the dock and beach. Walt even had the chance to reel in a small shark, but the line broke before he could get it out. Despite the fact he'd let the big one get away, Connor and I let him have a celebratory beer.

That was the beginning of our grand day, but as days tend to do, it kept on going. We came back home and threw the ball with Sam for a bit. Luckily, it didn't take him long to forgive us for leaving him behind.

Walt and I soon realized a nap was in order or we'd never make it to nightfall. Neither of us was accustomed to waking up at four-thirty, not even Walt. But after we had rested, we decided we would cook the newly caught fish, drink some beer, and play some checkers. I'll admit it was strange, but checkers had become the center of our friendship. You wouldn't think such a simple game would spring fourth all it did for the two of us, but while we played the best stories, discussions, arguments, jokes, and memories were shared between us.

As we'd done many times, we cooked the fish on my grill and ate as the night arrived. There was something mighty delicious about eating food that didn't come from the market, but maybe that was all in my head. After dinner we packed a cooler full of beer and ice and set up shop on Walt's porch, with Sam lying right next to the lantern at our feet. This was somewhere around the five hundredth game we had played, or at least kept score for. I knew that because we kept a tally on the wood floor of Walt's porch. In the corner, just beyond his back door, there were about two-hundred tiny knife marks carved into the wood under my name, and about three-hundred under Walt's name. Yeah, he was better than me.

But it wasn't the game of checkers I recall from that night. I was about to make a move in the midst of our second game, when I realized something about Walt that I hadn't before.

"Why are you always biting your fingers, Walt?"

At first he looked at me like I was crazy, then he chuckled.

"I don't even realize when I'm doing it anymore."

"Well?"

"I used to bite Olivia's fingers."

"Excuse me?"

He laughed again. "Whenever we were sitting around the house, or driving in the car, or anything else, really, we'd always hold hands."

"Yeah, I reckon that's pretty normal for two lovers to do. I don't know about this biting thing, though."

"I know, I know. For some reason I used to like nibbling at her fingers. It was just a stupid habit. I guess I started doing it to my own fingers some years back."

"Like you're a dog or somethin'?" I asked with a hoot.

"Actually, Olivia used to joke that I was part-Sam."

"Sam?"

"Yeah."

The dog lying next to us wagged his tail at hearing his name. I made a move in the game but my mind was muddled. Sam couldn't have been much older than six or seven.

"Ah, Walt?"

"Yeah?" he asked as he surveyed the board.

"How is it that Sam . . . ah . . ."

"Oh, right. Sorry. We had a dog named Sam when we were married, a yellow lab, like this guy here. He died about eight years after Olivia passed, so I went out and got another yellow lab, and for some reason, it felt wrong not to call *him* Sam."

"Oh."

"I've been doing this for a while now. This here is Sam the Third. Hopefully he'll be around until the end."

"The end?"

"Yeah, till I go see Olivia."

I looked down at Sam, who seemed to know he was being talked about. "What will you do with him when that happens?"

He looked at Sam, then back at me. "He seems to like you."

We played for a little bit longer, finishing our second game and getting into our traditional third and final game of the night. It was in the midst of that third game that Walt suddenly blurted out the answer to the question I'd been wondering about for years.

"Olivia died in childbirth."

I looked up at him, but he kept his eyes on the board. His face appeared as if he had said nothing at all, which had me wondering if it was only my imagination I had heard. "What's that, ya' say?"

"She died giving birth to our child. That's why she passed when she was so young."

"Oh." I leaned back in my chair. "I'm sorry."

"That's not why I told you. Sympathy doesn't do much almost half a century later."

He still hadn't taken his vision off the checker board.

"I's just being polite."

"I know."

"Then why'd you tell me?"

"I don't know, maybe I shouldn't have."

Walt made a quick move and sat back in his chair. He turned toward the sandy dunes and dark saltwater.

"No, no. If you want to say something, then say it. You ain't got to play tough with me."

"I just felt like telling you. I know you were wondering about it, and I respect that you never asked me after all this time. I've almost told you about twenty times, but something else always held me back."

I made a move and took one of his men, which made me feel guilty considering the circumstances. "I'd be lying if I said I didn't wonder about it."

Walt stared off into the distance of the waters, as if he had no intention of finishing the game.

"Walt?"

"Yeah?"

"You want to call this one quits."

"No," he said, leaning back up to the board. "Course not."
He made a move.

"So, what happened to the child?"

"That was the thing that held me back from telling you."

"Pardon?"

I moved one of my men but I could tell neither of us was
paying much attention to the game anymore.

"I guess I've already opened up enough to you." Walt
stood up and walked over to the edge of the porch, where he
sat with his back to me. "A couple months before Olivia was
due, the doctor told us there were some problems. It didn't
really surprise us 'cause she'd already had two miscarriages, but
this time the Doc told us that Olivia might be in danger. I
didn't much understand what he was saying, nor did she. But
all I heard was that giving birth to our child might put her
life in jeopardy. I'm sure modern medicine could've helped the
issue nowadays, but back then there weren't as many options
and we didn't know what to do. Abortion wasn't legal yet, but
there were places you could get it done, back ally clinic type
places. I wasn't one for killing my child, but I thought it should
at least be discussed. You know what I'm sayin', right?"

"Sure, 'course I do."

"But it was Olivia's baby and she wouldn't do it. She was
having that child no matter what. We fought about it for weeks.
I screamed at her, telling her we should just get rid of the baby
and try again to get pregnant. We could have more kids if she
was around, but we sure couldn't if anything happened to her.

That's the way I saw it. I ended up moving out for a bit, and when I moved back in I screamed at her some more. Heck, I nearly," he took a deep breath, "I nearly hit her one night I was so angry. But it was all about her safety," he pleaded as he turned back to face me. "I was so worried about her it drove me crazy."

"I probably would've felt the same as you," I assured him.

He turned back toward the beach. "Turns out the doctor was right. Half way through the delivery something went wrong. They made me leave the room; told me I couldn't be there. An hour later they came and told me . . . .they told me . . ."

He couldn't finish, so I stood up and joined him on the steps.

"They were surprised when the baby lived," he went on after collecting himself. "I had a little boy, they told me, as healthy as could be. They asked if I wanted to see him. I thought they were kidding. I was sure if I saw that kid I'd murder him right then and there."

"You wouldn't have done that," I objected.

"You never know what a grieving man will do, Buck. Sure, I knew it wasn't my boy's fault, but at the time that didn't matter. I told 'em I didn't want the kid and to keep him out of my sight. They asked about family who could care for him, but both my parents were dead and my brother had died in the war. Olivia never knew her dad, and her mom was already in a nursing home at the age of fifty-five, senile from some disease. Olivia had a sister but she lived up north and we never saw her; I wasn't about to burden her with a kid. So I left the hospital despite the nurses physically trying to keep me there, begging that I take my son home with me. God Bless 'em, they tried to talk sense into me. But I left and drank straight through for eight days until I woke up in a street gutter one morning. Not much after that I moved down to Edisto."

We sat quietly for nearly two minutes, with only the waves echoing through our ears.

"So you don't know what happened to your boy?"

Walt wiped at his eyes before answering. "About twenty some years ago, when my boy would've been around ten years-old, I worked up the courage to try to track down his whereabouts. I went back to the hospital and they sent me to the local orphanage where they said he would've been sent. I even went to an adoption agency in the area. But it was point-less. All I had was his birthday and the hospital where he was born, and those get lost in the shuffle with things like this. It would have helped if I'd taken the time to name him or sign some official paperwork turning him over to the State, but I think that was God's way of punishing me. Obviously he would've gotten a new last name if he was adopted, but it would've helped in looking back at the hospital and orphanage records. I was in such a hurry to push my boy away I didn't even give him the courtesy of a name. Some government worker probably had the honor of naming my child. How do ya' like that? And you know the worst part of it all? Going back and seeing the orphanage where he most likely grew up only made my guilt even worse. I wish I'd never gone at all. It was such a ghastly place. I don't mean any harm to the people running it, 'cause they just didn't have the resources and wherewithal to take care of so many kids. But the thought of my son being raised in such a place gives me nightmares."

"Are you sure they can't track him down?" I pleaded. "It seems like it'd be possible; technology's a lot better now than it was in the fifties and sixties."

"All the technology in the world can't make a miracle happen. I met a lot of nice people who tried to help me, but it's like searching for a needle in a haystack. Like I said, I don't have a name. I don't know what he looks like. I don't know for sure where they sent him or if a family ever adopted him. I don't know anything about him, other than his birth date, of course."

"And when's that?"

"September fifth, nineteen fifty-four. But the poor kid, or man, I guess I should say, probably doesn't even know that's his true birthday. One of the ladies at the orphanage told me some of the kids back then didn't ever know where and when they were born. Probably would nowadays, with stricter laws and more detailed reporting methods, but not in the fifties. Back then they just shuffled the orphans around to different places. It was a struggle just to keep them alive, much less track all their personal histories. Gosh, can you even imagine not knowing when your true birthday was, Buck? I know that's something trivial in the grand scheme of things, but that chokes me up every time I think about my boy."

I wanted to say something to comfort him, but I couldn't find the words.

"As the years have gone on, I've realized I can't change what I did. But that doesn't mean I forgave myself for abandoning my son and treating Olivia so badly in the last months of her life. When I play my violin each morning, I'm asking God and Olivia to forgive me. I ask God to let me have some kind of an effect on my boy's life in order to make up for what I've done."

"What do you mean, 'effect'?"

"I know it's damn near impossible, but a man likes to go to his grave knowing he helped his son in every way possible. For me, I just want to help him in *any* way possible. Olivia knows where our son is and I know she hears my prayers, so I hold out hope that one day I can somehow be a father to my son." He looked over to me. "You think that'll ever happen, Buck?"

"Sure, crazier things have happened."

He didn't seem to believe my words. "Let's postpone this game. I have to get up early tomorrow."

He walked back in his house with Sam following. I sat there on the porch for several minutes and stared out over the sea, the moonlight glazing the water like icing on a cake. I wished there was a way I could help my friend, but I was completely helpless.

8

WE WALKED toward the front of the small church with the two firemen leading the way. Out of habit, Peter and I both reached over to the Holy Water Font, but the water had evaporated. The tabernacle behind the altar appeared to be empty as well. Father Powell must have removed the Eucharist before locking the doors of the church. As we moved slowly up the center aisle, I felt as though the black suit on my body would melt at any point and burn my flesh. But despite the soaring temperature, the heat didn't seem to be affecting the structure of the church. The mahogany-paneled walls were not warped, the Stations of the Cross paintings had not melted in any way, and the stained-glass windows were not fogged or distorted at all. I didn't know how strange this actually was, but a part of me expected to see at least some effects from the temperature being over two-hundred degrees.

I tried to keep my wits about me, taking in everything I saw and processing information as best I could as we moved past the fifteen or so pews on each side. I couldn't write anything down at that moment, so I would have to mentally register my observations. I wasn't even exactly sure what I should be looking for, but I knew immediately that this was not some hoax and was anxious to relay that back to Father Chase in Worcester.

When we had reached the front steps leading up to the altar, Sergeant Hampton pointed toward the left side of the church. Peter and I took this as our cue to move past them. We hesitated, both waiting for the other to go first, before I gave in and led the way. Despite moving at a snail's pace, I was panting like a dog and sweating profusely. It was hard to ignore that the heat was becoming almost unbearable. They may have originally used some kind of tool or gadget to gauge where the heat was coming from, but anyone could feel the temperature rise in this part of the church.

Within a few seconds we had rounded a thick pole bracing the roof and came face to face with the statue, tucked away in a stone enclave on the front wall of the church. As with most statues of Mary, she stood straight up with her arms extended outward, as if waiting to embrace someone standing before her. She wore a white gown that stretched to her feet and a light blue robe thrown over it. Her face was familiar, as it always felt to me. A pool of wax was caked on the ground below a metal rack which normally would've held votive candles, one of the few signs that the heat was affecting something other than us. Two kneelers rested in front of the candle rack. I knelt down on one and bowed my head to pray. I expected Peter to do the same, but he didn't.

As I stood up, I watched Peter take a step toward the statue and reach for his gloves. I knew what he was thinking. I too felt the need to touch the statue with my bare hand, out of curiosity more than anything else. But just then we heard Sergeant Hampton's voice snap at us from behind.

"You can't do that!" He quickly approached. "Are you crazy? If you take those gloves off and touch the statue it will burn your skin off." His voice was muffled and sounded eerie through the mask.

"Can I touch it with my gloves on?" Peter asked.

"If you think you can stand within a few inches of that thing without backing away, give it a shot."

"We may have to move this statue," Peter replied, mainly talking to me. "We have to be able to approach it."

"You two can't move that thing. It's far too heavy."

"We realize that, Sergeant," I said to him. "I believe Peter meant higher authorities may have to come in and move it out. At some point we want these people to get back in their church."

Sergeant Hampton huffed as he stepped back. Peter and I moved around the metal candle rack and found ourselves at the foot of the statue. I recalled from many of my studies that Marian statue phenomenon's sometimes had photos to validate them, but I couldn't see any changes in appearance. A picture could not capture the temperature, and I wasn't even sure an ordinary camera would work in this heat.

Peter shuffled his way around to the back part of the statue and peered upward. He placed his hands on it to brace himself, but soon realized he couldn't keep them there. He quickly released his hands from the statue, instinctively waving them in the air. "Don't touch it, Paul. It's too hot."

I wanted to respond, but suddenly everything went black. Not a second later I felt myself fall into the candle rack behind me. I tipped it over and fell to the ground.

Peter scurried back around the statue and grabbed me. "Paul! Paul! Are you okay?"

I nodded but was too woozy to speak. The two firemen ran over and helped carry me to a nearby pew. I could instantly tell the difference in stepping back from the statue. It was at least twenty degrees cooler.

I could barely hear my own voice as I tried to assure Peter I was okay. "I'm fine. Really, I am."

"I knew we shouldn't have let anyone else in here," Sergeant Hampton said. "We need to get out of here."

"No," I fired back. "Don't say that. Let Peter go back to the statue."

Sergeant Hampton shook his head in frustration before walking away. When we were alone again, Peter said, "I don't even know what I'm looking for. What else should I do?"

"I don't know," I answered him. "We already know this is for real, and that's all Father Chase wanted from us. Just go back to it one more time and see if you can examine it or find anything out of the ordinary. Any information we bring back with us won't hurt."

He patted me on the shoulder and braced himself for another approach. But just as he took a step forward, I heard two noises: a humming jingle and a scuffling on the floor, both distant through the mask on my head, though I could tell Peter and the firemen had heard the strange sounds as well. We turned around, our stunned eyes met by a young man, no older than twenty or so, coming up the right-side aisle. His dress was plain, with a pair of jeans, ragged sweatshirt, a green, athletic headband gripping his forehead, and *no* protective suit. He swept the floor casually, as if nothing strange was taking place within the walls of this church.

"Hey, Donald!" Sergeant Hampton yelled. "What're you doing in here?" The boy did not flinch or acknowledge us in the least. He just kept coming up the side aisle, sweeping and humming his song all the while. "How did you get in here?" Sergeant Hampton barked as he made a move toward him.

I slowly found my footing and made my way over to where Peter stood at the end of the pew. "What's going on?" I asked. Peter didn't answer me. We watched as Sergeant Hampton and Burt eventually came face to face with the young sweeper. The Sergeant threw his hands up and questioned him again.

"How did you get in here, Donald, and how . . . how can you be in here without a suit?"

The boy finally stopped with his sweeping when he realized he could not move forward anymore. He tried to shift around the large man standing before him, but Sergeant Hampton would not allow it. The unexpected visitor rocked back and forth and swayed his head from side to side, never making eye contact. He began to moan and mutter senselessly.

"Can I . . . can I . . . I must keep it clean . . . . keep her home clean. Please . . . please . . . ."

"What're you talking about?" the Sergeant fired back. "You've got to get out of here."

As he and Burt went to grab him, the boy screamed.

"Please!! No, no! . . . I must . . . clean her floors. No!"

The two firemen threw the broom aside and dragged him against his will toward the back doors of the church. Peter ran down the center aisle. Not knowing what else to do, I followed. "Don't hurt him," Peter yelled as he approached them.

"He doesn't understand." The boy continued to scream hysterically. Again, Peter pleaded with them. "Stop it! Let him go!"

"Don't tell me what to do!" Sergeant Hampton yelled. "I don't care if he doesn't understand."

The Sergeant tried to give the impression he was in control, but I could see through his mask that the color had left his face. The mystery of this situation stole the strength from my legs as I followed the commotion to the exit of the church. Sergeant Hampton unlocked the doors and flung them open just as the frightened boy freed himself of their clutches. He awkwardly sprinted into the gravel parking lot straight to a waiting Father Powell. The elderly priest embraced the crying boy as he looked up at us.

I could tell by Father Powell's expression that there was more to this phenomenon than he had originally claimed.

9

I HAD a plan.

I hated lying to Walt, but I knew he wouldn't have approved of what I intended to do. So I told him I was headed to see my nephew for a few days. In truth, I headed clear across the state to Aiken, the town on the Georgia border where Walt's son was born. The drive entailed three hours of highway cutting between rows of corn, wheat and cabbage. I left early on a Wednesday morning in the spring of 1991, with the radio playing and a hot cup of coffee at my side.

My decision to meddle hadn't been instantaneous. After Walt told me the story of his son, I spent almost a whole year trying to think of how I could help. He did his best to convince me that he'd done everything he could to find his child, but I came to the conclusion that I couldn't live with myself if I didn't at least try to do my part. With great care and a bit of slyness, I got all the information I could from Walt. In a leather journal I had purchased, I wrote down the name of the hospital, the date and year his son was born, the orphanage in Aiken where the boy was most likely sent, and a few other bits of knowledge I thought could be helpful. Three different times

I set out to find the highway before turning around and returning home. I wondered what good my efforts could do for such a hopeless situation, and I also feared I would hurt Walt since I knew he wouldn't want me digging through his past. But still, my conscious wouldn't let me rest, and I finally did find the highway in April of 91.

I pulled off at the Aiken exit about noon on a warm Wednesday. It was a town surrounded by pristine horse pastures and a quaint Main Street lined with shops and restaurants. Before I could do anything, I needed to eat. I ventured in to the local diner and struck up a conversation with an elderly man at the next table who made me look like a young, spring chicken. I told him why I was in town and listened while he gave me directions to the hospital. I figured this was the best place to start.

When I walked into the hospital lobby, I approached the front desk and told the receptionist why I was there. She informed me with a polite but practiced smile that I needed to speak with someone on the fourth floor in the Social Services department, but before I walked away she asked me what year the child was born. When I told her, she laughed. "I'm sure they keep good records up there, but good luck with that."

One hour later, a man named John Hart in Social Services also turned up his nose at me.

"Nineteen fifty-four?"

"Yes, sir," I replied. "On September fifth."

"That was a long time ago. I'm not sure they really went the extra mile back then to keep track of stuff like this. Did you say you at least had the child's name?"

"I know his father's name. The fact I got his last name has to help, right? Or at least the last name the child would've had."

"Not necessarily. When a child is sent to an orphanage or a group home they often don't keep their family's name, that's what makes them orphans." I stared at him until he shuffled some papers on his desk to avoid my stare. "What was your friend's name?" he asked.

"Walter Henderson."

"Even if I could find something, we generally don't give out this kind of information to non-family members. You've got to know that."

"I understand, sir, however I sure would be grateful for any bit of information you *could* give me."

Mr. Hart took a deep breath. "I'll see what I can dig up if you want to come back tomorrow. In the mean time, I would go across town to the children's home on Bluff Rd. My secretary can give you the address. Today it's just a group home for kids we're trying to get out of abusive situations, but back then it used to be an orphanage and it was probably where your friend's son was sent. Maybe they'll have some records you can review."

"Home for Little Angels?"

"Yes," he answered. "How'd you know that?"

"My friend gave me the name of that home. He came up here in the mid-sixties to see what he could find. I was planning on going there when I left here, but I will need the address. I'll grab it from your secretary. Much obliged, sir." I stood up and shook his hand.

"If your friend already came here looking for his kid," Mr.

Hart said before I left his office, "what could *you* possibly do all these years later?"

I smiled and put my hat back on. "You never know what you'll find, I reckon. Thanks again, I'll see you tomorrow."

I left the hospital with directions to the foster home across town. I knew it had probably changed some since Walt visited over twenty years ago, but I assumed it would be in a poorer area of town based on what he'd told me. Turns out my assumption was right when I turned on Bluff Road and encountered abandoned homes, broken street lights, hungry stray dogs roaming the sidewalks, shady men standing on street corners, and buildings covered in graffiti.

Twenty minutes later, I had left the poverty-stricken neighborhood with nothing positive to show for it. An older lady had come to the door. She hadn't wanted to let me in and I couldn't blame her; she probably had strange men knocking on her door all the time. During our short conversation, I heard children running and screaming all about the house. I couldn't help feeling sorry for this lady. Her face and body looked as rundown as the home she ran. She explained that she had ten kids under her watch and she didn't have time to help me. She also informed me that the lady who'd run Home for Little Angels in the fifties and sixties, the wife of a Methodist minister and her aunt, had died, and the records from back then were probably lost along with her. And again, if I didn't have a name, what could I possibly hope to find?

I checked into a hotel across from the hospital, then ordered a pizza and ate it in bed. In my younger years I would've gone into the town in search of fun, but my bones were tired. As I ate my pizza and let the television pass the time, I began to wonder why I'd bothered with any of this. It was foolish to think I could stir anything up by coming to Aiken. I became frustrated with Walt. If only he'd given his son a name on the birth certificate, or actually signed some paperwork turning him over to the state instead of just walking out of the hospital and into the first bar he saw, there'd be some hope, some paper trail that we could follow. Going to the hospital with only his son's birthday just didn't seem like it would be enough, but I stubbornly hadn't let that set in my mind until I found myself in that motel room.

Eventually I drifted off to sleep on the lumpy mattress, only to be awoken in the early morning by a maid pounding on the door. After an awkward and brief exchange, I assured her I would be out shortly. I ate a quick breakfast and made my way over to the hospital.

I knew Mr. Hart would not expect me this early, but I didn't mind waiting. And wait, I did, for nearly three hours. It was past one o'clock when I finally got word from his secretary that he was ready to see me. The look on his face when I entered his office did nothing to boost my moral.

"Good afternoon, Mr. Washington. Did you enjoy your stay in Aiken last night?"

"Sure did. This was my first time coming here. You've got a great city to call home."

"It's really nothing special. Please, have a seat."

I sat in the seat opposite Mr. Hart's desk. I hadn't noticed it yesterday, but everything in his office was made of metal, including the desk, file cabinets, and bookcases. The floor was a bland, vanilla tile and he had no paintings or pictures on his walls. His hollow office made me anxious even in my own skin.

"I did some research this morning," he began, "and I still feel like you're reaching a little far on this."

"I understand," I assured him.

He opened a file and tilted it sideways, prompting me to lean up in my seat so I could look along with him. "This is a copy of the records of all the children born in this hospital in September of nineteen fifty-four. Because of our policies, I can't give you any family names, so I've blacked those out. But I can tell you that only four were not taken home by their birth parents that month."

"Only four, ya' say?"

"Yes, sir. Now, a lot of times the scenarios are completely different when things like this happen, just as they were back in nineteen fifty-four. Sometimes the family comes to the hospital knowing they don't want to keep the child, and hopefully they already have plans for what they want to do. It's nice to see the adoptive family come for the birth because you know that child is in good hands. But occasionally, we'll have a single mother, perhaps a young girl, who will sneak out of the hospital without her baby, just completely abandon it because she didn't want the child."

"That's terrible," I replied, even though I knew this was not much different than what Walt had done.

"It happens more than you'd think. In these cases, if we can't find next of kin, we can only sign the children over to the state, at which point they're sent to a group home where they're given names and taken care of until we can place them in a more permanent foster home or work out an adoption. Of course, that could be years later, especially back in the fifties when the procedures for these types of situations were a work in progress. Some kids may have spent five or more years at a place like the one you went to yesterday. Back then they were called orphanages and today group homes, but they're very much the same thing, or at least that's my own personal opinion. I assume you did make it over to Home for Little Angels?"

"I did. It was a very tough place to see."

"It is, but we're lucky it's there. Now, it sounds like your friend's case was a bit of a unique situation. You said he didn't want the child, but he didn't have an adoption set up?"

"That's right. He originally would've loved to have a son, so he definitely wouldn't have set up an adoption ahead of time. But his wife died in child birth, ya' see, and he resented the baby for what happened. He left in a fit of anger without taking the boy home or signing any paperwork."

"I see. What was her name? Henderson?"

I nodded. He flipped through another stack of papers, but gave me the impression I wasn't supposed to see what he was looking at this time. "Olivia?"

"That's right."

"Uh-huh, says she died in childbirth, but as you might expect, it says the child's name is unknown and it doesn't say where he was sent. In our current environment we'd have to report that information more strenuously, but as I told you yesterday, things weren't so efficient back then. I guess your friend's son could have been sent to the Home for Little Angels. I see here," he said, looking to yet another set of records, "we signed two boys over to the state in September of that year. What did they tell you over at the home? Did they have a record of any boys coming in around that time, or where they could have been sent once they received a new family?"

I sighed. "They couldn't help me. I don't think they really keep records over there at all. I got the impression that once a kid gets dropped off, they just make sure he doesn't die before a family can come and claim him."

Mr. Hart nodded. I was about to thank him and be on my way, but he had one last bit of information for me. "There was one other thing I found out from a little, tiny footnote on our papers from that year. I didn't even see it until a few minutes before you came in here."

"What's that?"

"Well, nowadays, children left by their parents are going to be sent to some kind of home within state lines. It just wouldn't make sense with funding issues and varying state laws to ship a kid born in South Carolina to a home in North Carolina or Virginia or wherever. It would cause too many complications. But it says here at the bottom," he continued, pointing to a paper in his file, "that from nineteen fifty to nineteen fifty-five, because of overcrowding, hospital authorities were allowed to send a child to this place outside Atlanta. I suppose with all those baby-boomers there were a lot of kids coming to us around that time, needing a home and an adoptive family. I don't know anything about this place, but they must have had some kind of program set up where our people here in Aiken could feed the kids into Georgia. Atlanta is such a big city that they may have had more places available for children like your friend's son, and it's really not that far down the road. I wasn't around, but I'm guessing things weren't as complicated back then, so sending kids across state lines wasn't as big a deal. They were just looking for anywhere a roof could be put over their heads. I'm not sure we could get away with that in today's environment."

Mr. Hart held out a sheet of paper and I looked at it. There was a name and address:

Sisters of Charity Orphanage
3434 Winding Grove Way
Sandy Springs, GA 30328

Walt had not mentioned this place when he told the story of trying to track down his son's whereabouts. Whoever had helped him twenty-five years ago must have overlooked what Mr. Hart had found.

"May I have a copy of this address?"

"You may, but let me warn you that I don't know for sure if the boy you're looking for was sent there. We just know it was an *option* during the year he was born. But of course, we also had options to send him across town or even somewhere else in the state that might have had an opening."

"I understand."

"And I don't have a phone number for this place or even know if it's still there. A lot of orphanages were shut down in the seventies, so it very well could be an empty building at this point." I sat still, waiting for him to write down the address. "But then again, maybe it's still there, just like Home for Little Angels here in Aiken is still around. And if it is there, maybe they'll have some information that could help you."

Mr. Hart wrote down the address for me and I thanked him. Back outside, I settled on a bench beneath an elm tree. Birds chirped, car horns sounded, and people walked by, all going about their lives as they did each day. But I ignored it all. I stared at the address in my hands as various thoughts ran across my mind.

I wondered if I could track down an Atlanta phone book or call information in search of the home, but something I'd never felt before churned at my insides, something that told me this adventure of mine was not quite over yet. It became clear that I had to journey to Atlanta and follow this lead. I had to actually go there and see what awaited me with my own eyes. Besides, I was a retired, old man, what else did I have to do this week? I reached for my keys, hopped in my truck and sought a west-bound highway.

10

I GATHERED my thoughts and emotions as best I could while Father Powell escorted the frightened boy to a nearby car. After removing his protective suit, Sergeant Hampton relocked the church doors before running into the parking lot, hollering and demanding that he be told what was going on. Burt followed his boss like a frightened puppy, still shaken by the incident. Fr. Powell gently placed the boy in the backseat and shut the door, then did his best to calm down both the firemen as he led them back towards their truck. I assumed the elderly priest was trying to give an explanation for this unexpected episode with the boy, but I couldn't be sure, as Peter and I were both still struggling to remove our own suits and remained perched on the church steps some twenty yards away. When we had finally shed them, I said, "Should we go over there?"

"I don't think so," Peter replied. "Let's wait here for Father Powell." I agreed with Peter as I took in the dumbfounded expressions of the firemen.

I turned toward the sea, noticing the dwindling daylight for the first time. A powerful wind flew in off the bay, chilling me as it dried my perspiration from earlier. We watched as the firemen packed up their things in only a matter of minutes and drove off, not even bothering to retrieve the suits Peter and I had worn. Father Powell left the boy in his car and approached us.

"Will you take a walk into the garden with me?"

We followed him around to the other side of the church, out of sight from the parking lot and through a set of white, garden gates. Father Powell led us to a pair of benches opposite one another where we all sat down, Peter and I on one and he on the other. A fountain rested between us with a faint trickle of lazy water falling into a gentle pool, barely heard over the crashing waves reverberating against the cliffs in the distance. A decorative street lamp rose up past our heads with ivy wrapped tightly around it, providing just enough light to make out our surroundings.

We waited for Fr. Powell to speak, but he didn't. He sat with his head down, his hands clasped together like he was praying. I didn't want to disturb him, but I couldn't stand the silence any longer.

"Is that boy okay?"

"He'll be fine. I gave him a book to flip through." Fr. Powell took a deep breath and finally raised his eyes to meet ours. "I'm sorry I didn't tell you about Donald. I planned on telling you eventually, but I didn't know he would be in there today."

"How did he get in there?" I asked. "And how did the heat not seem to affect him?"

"I can only answer one of those questions."

When he didn't go on, Peter said, "Please . . ."

"Donald is a good kid," he began. "He has something

called Fragile X Syndrome. Have you have heard of that before?"

Peter and I both shook our heads.

"I hadn't either, until I met Donald, but I still don't understand everything about it. The best I can tell you is that it's a little like Autism, and it tends to affect boys much more than girls. He struggles with some day-to-day things that we all take for granted. It's hard to get through to him, as I'm sure you just realized. He has to get to know you; that's why he panicked with the firemen."

"He seems to feel comfortable with you," I said. "How long have you known him?"

"Donald's been cleaning the church ever since I came to Jamestown five years ago, but it took about a year before he really let me in. I quickly realized that he's a patterned young man, which is another symptom of his syndrome. He often does the exact same thing every day, and that includes his cleaning regiment. Donald keeps his broom, mop, dustpan, and other supplies in a little room in the basement. The first day I locked the doors because of the statue, I was pulling out of the parking lot about noon and saw Donald crawling out of a hatch on the side of the church. My heart just about stopped when I saw him. I knew the vent was over there but never realized it led into his little room. I surmised he must have been down in the supplies room when I locked the doors. I should've thought of that at the time; he's down there every day. But in his own words, Donald explained that he'd found a way out through that hatch. At first I was relieved he'd gotten out, because I didn't know I had locked him inside. But it didn't occur to me until later that night that he didn't complain about the heat inside the church. I have no idea why it doesn't affect him."

"How do you think he got in the church today?" Peter asked.

"I assume he crawled in through the hatch. He must have remembered that it led into his basement supply room. From there, he just walked up the steps to the door that leads into the back of the church."

"But how did you not notice him coming in while you stood outside?" I asked.

"Donald gets to the church very early in the morning. His grandmother drops him off and he usually goes to work. Sometimes, though, he'll sit down in his room and read old gospel books and hymnals, or at least he pretends to read them; I'm not sure he understands what he's taking in." Father Powell paused in thought. "I guess no one was here when his grandmother dropped him off this morning. Donald must have discovered that the doors were locked and climbed down through the hatch. I told him he shouldn't come to clean the church until we figured out what was going on, but I guess he's been doing it anyway."

"What about his grandmother?" Peter asked. "Doesn't she know to keep him out of there?"

"No. She's not all there, if you know what I mean. Ironically, Donald's about the only one who can get through to her. I don't know where his parents are, but he's lived with his grandmother ever since I knew him. I told her to keep Donald away; I guess she just forgot. Her poor mind can't keep up with things anymore."

"Is Donald a parishioner?" I asked. "I mean, does he go to Mass? Or can he not really . . . ah . . ."

"I know what you mean," he answered, stopping me from finding a respectful way to finish my question. "Donald has been at every single Mass I've ever said at this church. He may be a little off in the responses at times, but he's always there, sitting in the front row. I've asked him why he comes so often and I think it's the pattern of the Mass; he says he likes how it's the same every time. I think coming here every day is something stable that keeps him on track. He doesn't go to school and this is his only job. I guess you could say he pretty much lives here at the church, down in that little room of his."

"Have you asked him about the heat?" Peter asked. "And why it doesn't seem to bother him?"

"Yes, I asked him. It's hard to get a clear answer from him, though. He says things in the church feel like they always do." Father Powell hesitated before going on. "But Donald knows about the heat even though he can't feel it."

"You mean because you told him about it?" I asked.

"Not quite." He rubbed his hands together as his legs jittered. "Look, I'm obviously a man of faith, but I don't want you to think that we're crazy here at this parish. I obviously believe in the things of the spiritual realm, but I hesitated to tell you about Donald because some of this is beyond my understanding. I don't know what to think."

"You need to tell us *everything*," I insisted. "We understand this is difficult, but nothing will get accomplished if we don't have all the information we should."

Father Powell stood up and walked over to a row of daisies, keeping his back to us.

"Donald says she talks to him."

"Who?" I asked.

"The Virgin Mother."

"As in, Mary, the Mother of God?" Peter asked rhetorically.

"He says when he's alone, sweeping the floors and wiping down the pews, she speaks to him through the statue." Father Powell turned to face us, but did not return to the bench. "I know how ridiculous this sounds, but I don't know what to think at this point because—"

"What does she say to him?" Peter interrupted.

"Lots of things, apparently. He says she's been talking to him for years. I never really paid much attention to him. Like I said, Donald is a good kid. He's never brought any harm to anyone. He's a simple boy and I felt he should be left alone. I thought if I told someone about this, they may take him away to a psychiatric ward or something. That would be the worst thing for him."

"Do you believe him?" I asked.

"Do I believe that the statue speaks to him?" I nodded. "I wasn't sure for the longest time. I never really had reason to ask myself if I believed him. If he thought Mary was speaking to him but he wasn't hurting himself or anyone else, why not let it be? But now things are different."

"Because of the heat?"

"Yes, but also because you showed up."

Father Powell looked in our direction, but not to me. He stared at Peter.

"What are you talking about?" Peter asked.

"A few weeks ago, Donald told me the statue had delivered him a message, but he comes to me a lot and says this. He usually either tells me the message was private and I can't hear it, or he does tell me the message and it just makes no sense. This latest message fell into the category of not making sense until the statue got warmer. And then I met you."

"You've got to explain yourself," I demanded.

Father Powell slowly walked back to the bench across from us and sat down. He delayed what he had to say as long as could.

"Donald claimed that Mary would warm the earth until a shepherd of the Church arrived in Jamestown, a shepherd made of the rock."

When he stopped, Peter and I sat still, not understanding. "I'm sorry," I said, "what does that have to do . . ."

I stopped as something occurred to me.

Peter frowned. "I hope you don't think that message was for me."

"Thou art Peter," Father Powell said with an uncomfortable smile, "and upon this rock I will build my church."

"I know the passage," Peter snapped.

"Look, I don't know what to think. When Donald told me this over a month ago, I brushed it off. How could that statement possibly mean anything to me at the time? But then I noticed the statue getting warmer and began to wonder. I told the parishioners about the statue and even joked about it with them. But I didn't tell anyone about what Donald had said. When the statue kept getting hotter, I called the Bishop and he informed me the next day that a Father Paul and Father *Peter* would be coming to investigate. I understand a lot of the things Donald says don't make sense, but doesn't this make you wonder?"

Peter tensed beside me. "I am not Peter the Apostle."

"But that is a strange coincidence," I interjected.

Peter glared at me in disbelief. "It's crazy to insinuate that this has anything to do with me. Even if we assume Donald is telling the truth, and even if we assume he is relaying the message correctly, no one will be confusing me with St. Peter any time soon. He's the rock Jesus spoke of, not me."

"If it was a divine message, you can't take it literally," I argued. "You have to try to understand the underlying meaning, sense the meaning, if you will. A perfect example is that Donald said she would 'warm the earth,' but the entire earth is not being warmed; only on these church grounds can the heat be felt. That's the way these messages are, if you believe them, of course. Besides, Donald said, 'made *of* the rock,' not *the* rock. Right?"

Father Powell nodded, but Peter pursed his lips and turned away from me.

I ignored him and pressed Father Powell. "You said Donald claimed Mary would warm the earth until a shepherd of the Church arrived in Jamestown; does that mean the heat will go away once that shepherd gets here? Did you ask Donald when the statue will stop doing this?"

"Yes, I asked him, but all he says is that the heat will remain until after *it* passes."

"After what passes?" I asked.

"I have no idea."

"Did Donald tell anyone else about this message? Or that he converses with the statue? Did you tell Sergeant Hampton about all this?" Father Powell shook his head to all my questions.

"I'm the only one Donald talks to. He may have mentioned it to his grandmother, but she wouldn't understand. And I knew the time wasn't right to tell Sergeant Hampton. I told him Donald must have been down in his supply room since morning, before we arrived here, but that I didn't know why the heat didn't seem to affect him."

"We should speak with Donald," I said. "Father Chase would want us to do that before we return to Worcester."

Fr. Powell hesitated. "Now might be a bad time. Perhaps I can take you over to his grandmother's house in the morning?"

Peter and I agreed to this plan but discovered that Father Powell wanted to take Donald home alone before returning to get us. He explained that riding in the car with strangers was the last thing Donald needed after the episode from earlier. We considered calling Mrs. O'Day for a ride, but decided not to disturb her so late in the evening. Instead, we would wait for Fr. Powell to return and pick us up.

Peter and I stood alone on the church steps in the midst of the darkness. The stars above us could be seen clearly against the black sky and the waves persisted with their rumbling into the cliffs below. I was on the verge of speaking with Peter about what we had just learned, but when I tried, he rose, cutting me off. He walked into the field on the east side of the church, approaching the cliff overlooking the water.

I could only wonder what he was thinking.

11

I GOT to Atlanta near dinnertime, too late to find the orphanage. If it was anything like the home in Aiken, I didn't want to go there after the sun had gone down anyway. Instead, I found another dingy motel and checked in. I knew it would be the kind of place I was looking for when I saw the fluorescent lights glowing from down the road; that usually meant it fell into my humble price range. I paid the overweight motel clerk his forty-nine dollars and journeyed up to my room where I took a long overdue shower. The warm water and hot steam soothed my muscles and turned my spirits for the better.

As a rejuvenated man, I went back into the city, stopping at a steakhouse where I sat at the bar and ate dinner. I tried to strike up a conversation with a man sitting a few stools down, but not with much success. I told him why I was in town and asked if he knew the best way to get to the orphanage in Sandy Springs. He said to head north on a nearby highway and I would be in the suburb in under thirty minutes. But he had never heard of any orphanage there and it was clear the conversation was over when he turned his head back towards the television. He made me realize why I tend to stick with small towns like Edisto. You could spark up a conversation with anyone there—stranger, friend, or foe. There simply wasn't enough going on in a small town to *not* take an interest in your fellow man's life. But here in Atlanta, where the people scurried around like ants, there was too much commotion to bother. I don't blame the big city folk; I think it's simply human nature to shut yourself off when you're surrounded by so many people with so many problems.

When I made it back to my room, I was asleep before I had closed the door. It was probably the first time in my life I was too tired to watch TV in a motel room. I even allowed myself to sleep to just past ten, when a maid woke me up by pounding on the door for the second day in a row. After a quick shower I thought about getting some breakfast, but I was hankering to get going so I headed north on an empty stomach, driving up the highway as the sunlight filtered its way through the cloud cover and shimmered across my windshield.

Not thirty minutes later, I clicked my blinker and got off at the Sandy Springs exit. I suddenly found myself driving through slow and pleasant neighborhoods, much different from the busy streets of Atlanta. Some of the homes were as big as any I'd ever laid eyes on, with perfectly groomed lawns and luxury cars in the driveways. I passed a park and then a school, both appearing like perfect places for kids to play and learn. I saw a nursing home, where I glanced at the old men sitting out front on rockers in the afternoon sun and wondered how long it would be before Walt and I found ourselves in such a home.

I pulled into a convenience store in an attempt to get directions. When I walked in, I knew this store had been around since the town had first popped up on the map. It looked like the type of place that would sell famous milkshakes and attract all the neighborhood children on their bicycles. No one stood at the checkout counter, so I wandered to the back and found a small deli stand. I knew my growling stomach was angry with me for skipping breakfast. To oblige it, I ordered a sandwich from a pretty, young brunette named Christina.

"I was wondering if you could help me find something in this area," I asked her as she made my sandwich.

"Sure, where ya' headed?" I handed her the piece of paper with the address of the orphanage. "Ah, yeah, I believe I know where this is. It's nearby, but let me think."

I almost jumped over the counter and hugged her at hearing that this place was not only still around, but could be just around the corner. Christina paused in making my turkey sandwich and looked to the ceiling. She mumbled under her breath and motioned with her hands like she was driving an invisible car.

"Okay," she finally said, "I'm pretty certain if you come out here on Henry Street, you'll eventually hit Harden Boulevard. Take a left on Harden, and after about five minutes you'll see Winding Grove Way. You'll want to take a right on that. But I'm not positive how long you're on Winding Grove before you get there. And I don't think it's an orphanage, by the way, like what you have written here," she said, looking back at the piece of paper. "I haven't driven by it in a while, but I think it's like, a daycare or something like that. But I know it's the same place 'cause it's run by those nuns. Not too many places around here are run by nuns," she added with a smirk. "I see them around town every so often."

I nodded, trying to retrace everything she had said. She

spoke too fast for my elderly ears and smacked on her gum as if her life depended upon getting the flavor out of it. I wasn't happy to hear the home was no longer an orphanage, but I knew I should be thankful that it was at least still there and run by the same group of women.

"You want mayo on this?" Christina asked, handing me back the address.

"Sure, only a bit, though. I'm mindin' my health."

She gave me a courtesy laugh and made the rest of my sandwich in silence. I thanked her when she had finished, for my lunch and for the directions. There was no place to sit in the store, so I ate my sandwich and chips in the car and washed it down with a soda as a breeze cooled me off through the rolled-down window.

When I had finished eating, I followed the directions I'd been given until I found Winding Grove Way. After a few miles, I wondered if the girl from the convenience store had been mistaken. I was suddenly in a wooded area, only seeing farm-like homes every so often. It seemed the town of Sandy Springs had thinned out to only trees and cows. But finally I saw a big wooden sign on the left side of the road: *Sisters of Charity—Home for the Children*. It was rustic, with a cross carved in the top and a quote on the bottom that read, "Let the children come to me." Bright, yellow sunflowers grew at the base of the sign and a few ferns were sprawled out around it. I pulled in the driveway that cut through the woods. On each side a thick forest stretched as far as I could see, with not the slightest sign of human activity. But I drove cautiously, thinking there may be kids running about.

After several minutes I moved through a large, stonewall

entrance with another cross on top of it, this one made of iron. When I entered the grounds I was surprised by what I saw. Unlike the group home in Aiken, this place consisted of several stone buildings rather than one rundown house. There were four structures of all different sizes built in a square pattern, with a courtyard in the middle. Unsure of where to go, I followed my nose to a parking lot behind one of the buildings and pulled into an empty spot. I climbed out of my car and looked around for someone who could help me. Not seeing anyone, I figured I better explore the grounds. I moved forward into the courtyard, reading the plaques just above the front door of each building. The largest structure was the dormitory, and the one across from it, the second largest, was a school of some kind. The other two buildings were a rec hall and a stone chapel.

As I meandered around, I became stunned by the lack of activity. Shouldn't I be hearing kids playing and running freely, or even nuns singing and praying? But there was nothing. Not knowing what to do, I hunkered down on a bench. It felt wrong barging into one of the buildings without an invitation. I knew I had to be careful in a place with so many children, me being a stranger and all.

It was nearly twenty minutes later when the doors of the chapel triumphantly burst open. Organ music erupted from within the stone walls, along with about thirty kids and several nuns. The children ran towards the rec hall across the courtyard, I assumed to eat some lunch or play games. The nuns tried to keep them in a straight line but it was more of a tsunami of toddlers and adolescents. A few of them glanced at me with curious eyes. I smiled and waved but most looked away.

I chuckled when some of the girls broke into cartwheels and a few of the boys pulled baseball cards from their pockets and began comparing them.

One of the nuns took note of me and came my way. She wore a black dress that stretched all the way down to her black shoes, and a black veil of some sort covered her head. A white border collar framed the veil and she wore a white undergarment beneath her dress that could only be seen up around her neck. My first thought was that she must have gotten hot in the summertime.

I removed my hat and stood up when she reached me. Alongside her she held a little boy by the hand. "May I help you?" I was distracted at first by the young toddler picking his nose, but I composed my laughter and answered her.

"Yes, ma'am. My name is Buck Washington. I was wondering if I could speak to whoever's in charge. I had some questions concerning someone who may have lived here many years ago."

"Do you mind waiting here in the courtyard while I let our Head Mother know she has a guest?"

"Be my pleasure. Thank you kindly."

She disappeared into the school with the little boy, still digging for gold up his nose. I returned to my bench, knowing I couldn't do much else. A few children walked about as I waited, some with an adult, and some who appeared old enough to mind after themselves on their own.

Finally, an older nun emerged from the school doorway, waving to me with a pasty white hand. She had a white sweater draped over her habit, but otherwise looked the same as the others. I had expected her to be wearing something else if she

was the head of this place, but what did I know about the hier-
archy of nuns?

"My name is Sister Marie Joseph," she said extending her
hand. "Was it Mr. Washington?"

Short as she was, I had to lean down to shake her hand. I
thought she may have been taller in her younger years, but her
elderly body looked like a candle that had been lit for a long
time and lost its wax.

"Yes, that's right," I replied. "But please, call me Buck."

"Alright, Buck. What brings you here today?"

"I wondered if we could go somewhere and talk for a
moment. I've got a question, but it's more of a story."

She smiled. "Everything you see here moving on two feet
is a story, Buck. But of course we can talk, that is, if you don't
mind walking to the playground with me. One of my sisters has
fallen ill and I must take her afternoon shift of watching the
young ones while they play."

I agreed and walked alongside her through the stone
buildings to a dirt path leading into the woods. We spoke casually at first, with her asking most of the questions. She asked all
about me: if I had family, where I was from, and what profes-
sion I'd spent my life working in.

In the distance I could hear children laughing and playing, and soon we had reached a small playground. It was deep
within the woods, surrounded by several weeping willows.
The clearing held slides, sandboxes, monkey bars, a miniature merry-go-round, and a colorful jungle gym. Sister Marie
walked over to a bench and relieved the nun who had been
there watching the ten or so children. After she had departed
down the path, Sister Marie and I sat down. Behind us there

was an ivory statue, maybe the size of my torso, resting on a gray, rock base. It was a lady dressed in a white robe, with her hands folded together and her feet standing on top of a snake. Her position behind us made it seem she was about to join our conversation.

"Is this Mary?" I asked.

"It is."

"Seems like she'll be listening in on us," I said with a nervous chuckle.

"She's always listening in on us. Now what can I do for you?"

"Well, I understand this place used to be an orphanage? Is that right? Or . . . I mean, is this still an orphanage? A girl in town told me she thought it was a daycare."

Sr. Marie laughed. "Is that what they think this place is now; a daycare? I suppose that is a good enough term for our modern world."

"I'm sorry. I didn't mean to offend you."

"No, you're actually right; this did used to be an orphanage. In a way it still is, or at least that's how I look at it. Terminology changes all the time in our society but the point of this place has been the same for almost a hundred years. You see, I came here in September of 1954, when this place was a home specifically for orphans. About fifty to one hundred children lived here for various lengths of time, children who had been abandoned by their birth parents for whatever reason. We took care of them, fed them, gave them shelter, and taught them school lessons if they were old enough. We helped find them families through adoption, which was always bittersweet. The sisters fell in love with those little orphans, especially the ones who stayed here for several years. But in our hearts we knew they needed a family, and it was our duty to help find them one."

"So when did things change?"

"To be honest, I'm not certain of when things began to change. I find my mind to be tired these days."

"I know the feeling."

"I believe it was in the seventies that our country's social policies changed and we moved to a line of thinking that children should be in foster homes or foster families rather than an orphanage like this. Don't ask me why people started thinking that; we took care of the little ones just fine. But some battles are out of my hands. Over the years we've adapted to what God calls us to do. To this day we sometimes still have an infant who needs a home for a while, and they will live here with me and the sisters for as long as they need to. Others are children whom the State has taken out of an abusive home and are only here temporarily until a better situation can be found for them, and still others are local kids whose parents just struggle through the day-to-day battle of raising their children and look to us for help. Or rather, when I say local, I mean from inner-city Atlanta. We have a daily bus one of the sisters drives. It shuttles the children to and from a downtown church in the morning, afternoon and evening."

I grinned at the thought of a nun driving a bus.

"The local kids sometimes come here because both parents work and the child just needs supervision for a while, but most often it's because the parents know their child will get a warm meal and a safe place to rest their head, not to mention some tutoring from us."

"Shouldn't some of these kids be at school right now?" I asked, looking at my watch.

"We only have a few locals here right now; more should be arriving later today in the afternoon bus. But to be honest, yes, some of them should be at school. But often when we take them home at night there's no one there to pick them up, so the sisters must bring the children back here to keep them from sleeping on the street."

I looked at the children playing before me and tried to picture them sleeping on the streets.

"I assume these parents don't pay you?"

"Oh, no, of course not. These are adults who can barely put food on the table for themselves, much less their children."

"Then who pays for this, if you don't mind me asking?"

"Well, thankfully this land was purchased by the Church decades ago for a very cheap price, which was a huge blessing. But as far as our day-to-day operations, we get most of our funds from contributions, and we get a lot of help from the Catholic Social Services group in Atlanta. They help raise money for us through golf tournaments, auctions, dinners, and other things like that. I try not to worry about money because I know we're doing the Lord's work. He will provide for us."

"You really are doing a great thing," I agreed. "No question about that."

"Thank you, Buck. Donations are always welcomed if you feel that strongly about what we're doing." I laughed at her wit. "But you still haven't told me why you're here," she went on, "unless you just wanted a lesson on the history of orphanages."

She listened intently as I told her the story of Walt and his son, and my trip to Aiken before coming to Atlanta, never once letting her eyes drift from my own. We both had a chuckle at the coincidence of Walt's son being born the same month she arrived here in Sandy Springs, but couldn't find any reason on why that might help. It took me nearly twenty minutes to explain the situation.

"What do you think, Sister? Do you think you can help me? Do you think you have some records you can review?"

"Yes, of course we have records, records of where these kids came from and records of where they're sent when they leave. And they've gotten better in the last few years as we've reached the computer age. A lack of records is not the problem."

I hung my head. "I know. I don't have a name. I can't believe I've tried to do this without a name."

"Yes, your not having a name doesn't help, but it does not surprise me either. Probably half the children back then came to us without a name. The other sisters and I were given the honor of naming those children. We usually went with apostles names for the boys and saintly names for the girls," she said with a bit of laughter as she reminisced. "But here is your other problem. You said the boy was born in September of nineteen fifty-four and could have been sent to us from the town of Aiken. I probably could look back in our files and find some helpful information, but very rarely was an infant sent to us in the same month in which he or she was born. Some of the kids we got were anywhere from three months old to a year when they arrived, sometimes even older than that. Unfortunately many of them lived other places and were passed between different government-run homes before they ended up here. So with that in mind, and the fact that you don't have a name,

I don't see how I can be of much help. The boy you're try-ing to find could have been sent to us from South Carolina in the mid-fifties. Lord knows we received children from all over back then. But he could have arrived at any point in a maybe a two or three year span, and if he did arrive here later in his life, he would've arrived with a name he received from somewhere else, which you of course don't have. I wouldn't be surprised if we received over fifty boys in that time frame, whether they had a name or not. It would just be too hard to track."

"I understand," I replied as I looked out toward the sur-rounding forest. "I don't even know for sure if Walt's son was sent here. I was just followin' a hunch."

As our conversation found a pause, one of the little girls riding the merry-go-round got off and approached us on the bench.

"Sister Marie!" she said with a burst of energy. "I hurt my knee."

"You did? Let me take a look."

Sister Marie bent down and grabbed the girl's leg. As she examined the small scrape, the girl eyed me. "Who's this, Sis-ter Marie?"

"This is my friend. His name is Buck. Would you like to introduce yourself?"

"Hi," she said, her voice as soft as a nightlight.

"Hello," I replied with a big grin. "What's your name?"

"Magdalene."

"What a pretty name."

"What's he doing here?" she asked, looking back to Sister Marie.

"He's trying to find out if one of his friends lived here

many years ago, and I'm trying to help him." The Head Mother took a Band Aid from her pocket and placed it over Magdalene's cut, then kissed the injured area. "Now, you go back and play."

Magdalene bent down and reviewed the work Sister Marie had done on her knee. Approving of the care she'd been given, Magdalene took off toward the sandbox. But she turned around one last time before leaving. "I hope you find your friend, Buck."

I smiled. "Do you always keep Band Aids in your pocket?" I asked the nun sitting next to me.

"Ever since 1960; I go through about a box a week." We both laughed. "Look, Buck, I have great sympathy and admiration for what you're trying to do. I feel your efforts to find this boy, or young man as he would now be, may end without the results you're looking for, but perhaps there is another reason you're here today."

"What do you mean?"

"The Lord works in mysterious ways. That is perhaps the most commonly used expression I've ever heard, but it is also the most accurate. Something brought you to our home today, Buck. I have no idea what it is, but it was *something*."

I thought about her words, turning to the statue behind us before returning my gaze to Sister Marie. "There's something I may want to do before leaving," I said, even surprising myself a little. "Can I come back in about thirty minutes and meet you again."

Sister Marie looked at her watch. "Most of the children will be doing their afternoon study hall by then. I suppose you can meet me in my office."

I shook her hand and jogged away, down the dirt path that had led us to the playground. I hopped in my car and a few minutes later I was back in the convenience store.

"Did you find those nuns?" Christina asked from behind her deli stand.

"Your directions were perfect. Thanks again."

I made a simple purchase and found my way back to Winding Grove Way. After getting some help, I arrived at the door of Sister Marie's office. She sat behind her desk grading papers with a red pen. "Looks like they made a lot of mistakes," I said, tongue-in-cheek. "You sure you're teaching these kids properly."

She lifted her head and smiled. "Well, we do our best. But we aren't helping raise these children to get into Harvard; we're raising them to get into heaven."

"Not a bad goal," I replied.

"What did you buy?"

I reached into my plastic bag and pulled out a yellow, disposable camera.

"I don't know if it will make Walt feel any better," I began. "But he's told me how bad it pains him to think about his son growing up in that run-down home in Aiken. I figured . . . well, I figured if I showed him how nice this place is he might be comforted by the thought that maybe his son grew up here. Even though this place has changed some since then, you said what's going on here is pretty much the same, and it looks the same as it used to, right?"

"It very much does," she replied. "I understand what you're trying to do. Would you like me to walk around the grounds with you?"

"I'd appreciate that."

We walked outside to the courtyard and began to take pictures. She pointed out a few of her favorite scenes, including the chapel garden and a fountain built in front of the dormitory. I took about ten pictures of the grounds, but then realized I had one more left to take.

"I hope you don't mind, Sister Marie, but I need you to be in one."

"Me?" she asked with a hoot of laughter. "Why on earth do you want me in one of these?"

"You're the one who would've raised Walt's boy, if he lived here, that is. Walt needs to see how nice you are. Of course I'll have to tell him that, along with the picture, but you know what I mean."

"All right, all right. Where do you want me?"

"Why don't you sit on that bench in the courtyard, where I was when we first met?"

We found our way over to the bench so she could sit down. I crouched to the ground, trying my best to get one of the stone buildings in the background. I counted down from three and snapped the photo. Sister Marie rose from the bench and stood next to me as several children moved by in a straight line, being led by one of her fellow sisters.

"You know, one thing struck me about your story, Buck."

"What's that?"

"Your friend's wife knew she was in danger by giving birth to her baby, but she still chose to give life to her son." I nodded but wasn't sure where she was going with this. "Sometimes I think orphanages are a thing of the past because of social policies and how things have changed, but other times I think it's because we've changed what we do when we don't want a child. I don't know if you friend's son has led a good life, but at least he was given the chance God intended him to have."

I now knew what she was getting at, and for some reason the little girl from the playground popped into my mind. I couldn't help thinking how difficult Magdalene's life probably was, but she knew what it felt like to be cared for, like she was when Sr. Marie placed that Band Aid on her cut and kissed her knee. Not everyone gets the chance to feel that. I was surprised when I felt my eyes water.

Sr. Marie was right to admire Olivia, and the elderly nun had helped me realize Olivia deserved my admiration too.

I turned and hugged Sr. Marie, probably holding on to her for longer than she expected. About five hours later, I was pulling back into my driveway in Edisto, tired as an old Hound dog.

12

I REMAINED on the steps of the church and waited for Peter to return for fifteen minutes, but realized he intended to stay out by the cliff. I crossed myself, walked into the grass pasture and stood beside him. We stared out over the dark ocean and the vast, night sky. A few glittery stars and a thumbnail shaped moon provided us with enough light to see the shifting water below. After a few seconds spent in silence, I said, "Did I ever tell you when I knew I was destined to become a priest?"

"I think so," Peter replied, turning to me for the first time. "When you visited Fatima with your family in high school, right?"

"That was what first inspired me, but I still had some doubts after coming back from Portugal. It was about a year later when I knew."

"I'm not sure I've heard this, then."

I put my hands in my pockets to shield them from the chilly wind. "I used to love being an altar boy," I began, "even when I was very young. It felt right to be so involved with the Mass, and I took pride in serving. But I especially loved to serve at midnight Mass. I thought that was the most peaceful experience, with the quiet anticipation, the Christmas songs sung by the choir, and the decorations all over the church. It was my favorite night of the year."

"I think Christmas Eve is a lot of kids' favorite night of the year," Peter said, a drop of sarcasm in his tone.

"True, but I like to think I was focusing on the right reasons to appreciate the night." Peter didn't respond. "Anyway, normally my family went to midnight Mass, but the Christmas after we returned from Portugal, my mom decided she was too old to stay up that late. I asked to go serve at midnight Mass, but my mom said I had to go with the family the next day. I didn't want to cross her, obviously, but I was going to serve at midnight Mass no matter what."

"So what'd you do?"

"A few weeks before Christmas, I signed up to serve without telling my mother. I went up to my room about ten-thirty on the twenty-fourth. Once my parents had gone to sleep, and once I had sworn my brothers to secrecy, I climbed out on the roof through my bedroom window and made my way down a ladder I had set up earlier in the day. I rode my bike to church in the middle of the night, served as an altar boy at midnight Mass, rode my bike home, and snuck back into the room using the ladder again."

Peter reviewed the story in silence before responding. "So you snuck out of your house in the middle of the night, against your parents' wishes, to go to church?" I nodded. Seconds later Peter couldn't help but chuckle and I joined in his laughter. "I think most kids were sneaking out to drink beer at that age," he added.

"Probably, but that's how I knew I was meant to be a priest."

My story had served its purpose, loosening Peter's mood. "So what do you think about all this?"

"I don't know."

I turned toward him. "You've got to think something."

"So do you," he fired back as he bent down to pick up a rock. "Why don't you ask yourself what you think this all means?"

He threw the rock into the ocean. Despite not being able to see it in the darkness, we didn't speak until we felt it had landed in the sea.

"Well, I do have thoughts. But I'm not the one—"

"You're not the one named Peter, the shepherd made of the rock, right?" I didn't answer him, but we both knew he was right. "Think about the absurdity of all this," he went on. "Do you really think this statue is speaking to that kid? How would the rest of the world view the Catholic Church if we told them this handicapped boy is speaking with the Mother of God through a concrete statue? That's not fair to Donald, but that's reality. And perhaps Donald did quote scripture concerning Saint Peter. So what? Never underestimate the power of a coincidence. Maybe one of the parishioners is named Peter."

"But one of them wouldn't be a 'shepherd of the church.'"

"Maybe one of them is thinking of becoming a priest; I don't know. But nothing a statue does inside that church has anything to do with me. Don't forget I'm not even supposed to be here. I'm only here to chaperone you."

"You're still here, Peter. Who cares how you got here? I don't see how you can say for certain that this has nothing to do with you. And you can't deny the heat inside the church. Isn't that amazing? And did you notice the heat hasn't affected the wood paneling or the paintings? It's unheard of for a painting to not be affected when it sits in such high temperatures like that. How can you explain that?"

"I don't know if I can explain it, but if the heat is being caused by something beyond this world, then it only frustrates me, not inspires me."

"How do you mean?"

"These poor people can't even go inside their own church," he snapped. "You heard Mrs. O'Day and Father Powell; they're terrified. Why would God do this? At first I was intrigued, but after going in there it only makes me angry. I know you don't like hearing me say this, Paul, but that's the way I feel."

"You don't think this could be some kind of miracle?"

"No. What good has come from it? Has God or the Virgin Mary blessed these people by keeping them from their church and scaring them half to death?"

"I don't know if I can claim they've been 'blessed,' but something is happening here, and we should—"

"Can we just stop talking about it?" he interrupted. "I told you before, I made a commitment to Father Chase to investigate this, and that's what I'm going to do out of respect for him. But I'm beginning to see more and more that I need to move on when we get back to Worcester. Just look at how different we're viewing this situation; I'm not meant to be priest."

When I saw that our focus had shifted away from the statues and toward Peter, I leapt at the opportunity. "Why can't you tell me more about your past? I can't get through to you if I don't know what originally caused your struggles. Why did you run away from your family? What happened before your time spent on the streets?"

"I told you before, that's not relevant."

"It *is* relevant. You're upset with God for the many struggles of your life, and you told me you've tried to make sense of everything that happened. But all your time spent on the street and your issues with drugs would've never come about had you not left home."

"It would've been worse had I stayed home."

"Why? Why do you say that? Were you abused?"

Peter turned his back on me, walking alongside the edge of the cliff.

I followed him. "I'm not going to let this go, Peter. I know it must be something awful if you want to wipe away all these years in the priesthood just like that. You've become a completely different person. Why do you want to leave it all behind? Why now after all this time? Tell me!"

Peter whipped around. "You don't want to know! No one wants to know what it's like to be abandoned! To be left at an orphanage for ten years, waiting and praying every night for a family to come and take you home!" He continued to walk toward me, pushing me back over my startled feet and screaming just inches from my face. I was so taken aback by his sudden rage I forgot we stood several feet from a treacherous cliff. "Or *is* this what you want to hear, Paul? Do you want to hear that when a family finally did take me home, my adoptive drunk of a father beat me senseless each night! Yeah, that's right; I was abused, just like thousands of other children across the world. Why do you suppose that happens, Paul? Now that you know, what will you do to fix it all? What will you do to fix me? Do you want me to go on? Do you want to hear that they treated me like a slave instead of a son? That the only reason they got me was to work me to death in their fields? Do you want to hear that I still have nightmares reliving the beatings I received as a boy? What is it that you want to hear? Please, tell me!"

I fumbled a response even I could barely understand. "I . . . I . . . I don't know. I'm sorry, Peter. I do want to hear. I want to help."

"I don't want your help!" He backed away, releasing his vengeful gaze. Both of us took several deep breaths. For nearly a minute, we didn't speak. When the intensity had settled, Peter went on, now in a calmer voice, a tired one, with his back to me.

"I lived with nuns for the first ten years of my life, Paul. They said that God loved me, and that I was one of his special children. They said I should pray to him each night. So I did. I prayed for a family, one that would actually want me, unlike the one that gave me up. Eventually, he answered those prayers by sending me an abusive, alcoholic father and a mother who hated me. So I prayed some more, trying to understand why I was being put through such anguish. But the anguish didn't stop, and I lived through an adolescent hell for eight years."

"That's horrible, Peter. I don't know what to—"

"But I finally gained the courage to make a run for it, and I ran right into a life in the gutter, saved only by the grace of an elderly nun who remembered me from my days at the orphanage. If it wasn't for Sister Marie I probably would've ended up dead or in jail, and I was well aware of that. When she started talking about the priesthood, I felt guilty for not following that path. I felt like I owed her. So I made the ridiculous decision of becoming a priest. I thought at the worst it would keep a safe roof over my head. All that stuff I told you back in Worcester about making sense of my suffering was just to make my troubled faith sound poetic. It was bull. I became a priest because of pressure; pressure from my troubled surroundings and pressure from a nun who brainwashed me into thinking this life would help me make peace with God."

"That's not fair, Peter. You just said Sister Marie saved your life by taking you in. The God she loves and serves lived through her decision to do that. I'm sure she didn't brainwash you. She was just trying to pass on that love because she thought it would help get your life back on track."

He finally turned back to face me.

"Okay, if you have all the answers, let's get back to this statue. Why is this happening? Why is God terrifying these people with such an enigmatic and frightening situation?"

I sighed. "Obviously I don't know, Peter."

"Surprise, surprise."

"We have to give it time," I argued back, ignoring his sarcasm, "that's the way life works. We can never understand things in God's time, but some day we will. Some day we will know why this phenomenon is happening, and some day you will understand why God put you through all that suffering. I can't promise when, I can only promise that you will. I understand it doesn't make sense for God to keep these people away from their church, just like it doesn't make sense that he loves all his children and yet some are destined to suffer for their entire lives. It'd be nice if we could find answers to all these troubling questions just around the corner, but things don't work that way."

"Yeah, instead he has to heat a statue, scare a bunch of people and let a babbling retard speak for him."

My body felt like it would drop to the ground. I couldn't believe Peter would say such a thing. It didn't matter what his childhood was like or what his feelings toward God were. There was no need to disrespect Donald this way.

"I'm sorry," he said, before I could condemn his comment.

I decided I would rather move on than accept his apology on behalf of Donald.

"You know, to me it makes sense the statue would speak to him."

"How's that?"

"Think about it. The mentally challenged are at times the most Christ-like. They don't judge; they don't condemn; they aren't wrathful; they often love more than we possibly could. Their innocence is as pure as the Virgin Mary. Why shouldn't she seek a soul like Donald's? Maybe she sees a little bit of her son in him."

Peter merely nodded and gave an uninterested grunt. He walked away toward the gravel parking lot. I followed him, but we waited for our ride a good twenty strides apart.

Standing alone, I thought back to last week, realizing now why that orphaned girl in Costa Rica had brought back Peter's bitterness. He saw himself when he looked upon her, and for that reason I found myself wishing he'd never met her.

The glow of Father Powell's headlights approaching from the distant road met our faces a few minutes later. He drove us back to Mrs. O'Day's house and made plans to pick us up after

breakfast. We used her key to let ourselves in. Finding her bedroom light on, we thought about telling her we were home, but
decided not to disturb her. Instead, we walked into the kitchen
where we found a note sitting on the counter informing us
there were two sandwiches waiting in the refrigerator. We ate
them together in silence before Peter sulked his way up to one
of the guest bedrooms and shut the door. I stayed downstairs
and studied some of the books I had brought with us, and the
notes I had taken throughout the day. I spent an hour doing
my best to make sense of what was happening here in Rhode
Island, but by eleven o'clock, exhaustion consumed me.

The next morning, Mrs. O'Day fixed us a feast: scrambled
eggs, Belgian waffles with maple syrup, bacon, fruit, and fresh
orange juice filled with pulp. The same classical radio station
she had listened to in her car played throughout her house stereo speakers. As we listened to the music and ate our breakfast,
she did most of the talking, much like she had done the day
before. But I didn't mind her chatter; I was not prepared to be
alone with Peter.

Father Powell called and said he would be a little later
than he had anticipated. Mrs. O'Day was thrilled by this news,
realizing she got to keep her company a little bit longer. Her
loneliness was obvious, seen clearly in her body language.
She talked of her late husband constantly, with a smile, but
one cloaked in pain. I learned they were never able to have
children, and she confessed her regret of not having looked
into adoption before he got sick. I thought of Peter's words
the night before, how he questioned why God would scare
this parish. I wondered the same thing. This woman had

experienced enough sadness and confusion in her life. Why was this happening?

While we waited for Father Powell, she took us on a walk into the woods behind her home and showed us a hawk that had become an unexpected companion of hers. "You must be completely still," she pleaded with us. "He's as big as a cat, but he's easily frightened." Peter and I stood motionless, glancing up about twenty yards into a pine tree. "I've been coming out here almost every day since Bobby died," Mrs. O'Day whispered without taking her eyes off the hawk. "He used to love to take walks in these woods."

Suddenly, the hawk took off from his nest.

"Oh!" Mrs. O'Day pointed. "There he goes!" Our heads tilted back, watching as the hawk climb above the tree line with his massive wings. I glanced over to Mrs. O'Day, enjoying her excitement just as much as watching the bird.

When Father Powell arrived, we hopped in the car with him and made our way to Donald's house.

"Don't expect Donald's grandmother to welcome you with open arms," he said as he turned out of the neighborhood.

"She's not too friendly?" I asked.

"No, she just doesn't realize when people are around sometimes. And as far as Donald goes, treat him as you would anyone else. He seems to respond to people who don't talk down to him."

"That makes sense," I said. Peter sat in the back and hardly said anything for the ten minute car ride. His behavior was changing more and more by the hour, and I could tell Father Powell had taken notice of Peter's detached mood when he began directing all his conversation toward me without even considering Peter's presence.

We arrived at a small brick home in the back of a cul-de-sac. It looked similar to Mrs. O'Day's house, but the exterior was not well kept like hers. The grass was tall, weeds grew in the cracks of the sidewalk, and shutters hung loose off the side of windows. Father Powell walked into the home as if he lived there, without knocking on the door or ringing the doorbell.

"Donald?" he yelled. "Mrs. Devonshire? Anyone home?" We followed him into the house, making our way through the kitchen. Dirty dishes, empty bags of chips and soda cans were scattered all over the place. The tile floor was sticky and the stovetop was caked in some kind of crusty food. Father Powell threw his hands in the air. "I came here last week to clean this place. Look at it now."

We moved into the den where a small TV was tuned into a talk show. Three people with tattoos and piercings were screaming at one another about who was the true father of a child. I watched as obscenities flew from their mouths like bees from a beehive. But even worse, there were rows of people standing in the crowd cheering them on. Why would people encourage this hate? Better yet, why was this entertainment? I could only feel sorry for the child who was sitting backstage, shown in a small box at the bottom of the screen. Or perhaps I felt sorry for all of them.

"Hello, Mrs. Devonshire," Father Powell said.

I glanced around the room. It wasn't until I saw where Peter's eyes were pointed that I realized there was someone on the couch: an elderly, feeble lady, buried beneath blankets and pillows. Only her head and short, white hair were visible.

Father Powell walked over to her and crouched down. "These two men have come from Massachusetts to visit Donald. They're here about that statue at the church. Do you remember me telling you about that?" She didn't react much, only a moan and a nod as she kept watching the TV. "Is Donald upstairs?"

His question was answered by a thumping noise from the floor above. It was a constant sound, with only a second between each thump.

Father Powell glanced up at us. "Sounds like he's in his room." We walked up the steps, past the clothes lying on the floor and the sports magazines spread everywhere. Father Powell walked straight up to one of the bedroom doors and knocked.

"Donald? You in there? It's me, Father Powell."

We heard heavy, rapid footsteps approach the door. Donald swung it open and embraced Father Powell with his free hand. In the other hand he held a basketball. "Hello, Fader Powell!"

"Hey buddy! Are you working on your dribbling?"

"Yep, yep. Workin' on my dribblin'!"

Donald moved back into his room and attempted to dribble the basketball through his legs, though not with much success. He was wearing green athletic shorts and a small, white T-shirt. He also wore the same green headband from the previous day. The three of us moved into the room. Donald picked up his ball and backed away from us.

"Who them, Fader Powell? Who them, Fader Powell?"

"These are my friends, Father Peter and Father Paul. They

have come to talk about the statue at church. Would you mind answering a few questions?"

Donald didn't answer. He swayed back and forth, keeping his eyes away from us and glued to the ceiling.

"Why do you wear a headband, Donald?" I asked him. He reached up and patted the green cloth gripping his forehead, as if to ensure that it was still there. He pointed to a poster above his bed of a professional basketball player. This same player was posted in a variety of other places throughout Donald's room. For the first time I noticed his headband had a Boston Celtics' emblem on it. "So you like Larry Bird, huh?" I asked, looking back to the poster. Donald nodded but still didn't look at me. "We're from just outside of Boston," I told him. "We've both seen Larry Bird play." Donald's face brightened with color and his fingers gripped the basketball tightly. He finally made eye contact with me, but only for a second. "Have you ever seen him in person?"

You could tell Donald wanted to answer but was still uncertain about the situation. "Donald absolutely loves Larry Bird and the Celtics," Father Powell said on his behalf. "He never misses a game on TV, but I don't think he's ever had the chance to see them in person."

Donald shook his head.

"One of the assistant coach's sons is actually in my class," I said. "Maybe we can work something out and get you to a game."

At hearing this, I thought Donald might leap out his second story window.

"Wouldn't that be great, Donald?" Father Powell asked, answered shortly thereafter by Donald vigorously nodding his head. "Well, you better be nice to my friends, then. They won't want to take you to a game if you aren't helpful. Why don't you sit down, buddy?"

Father Powell waved him into a chair by a brown desk covered in various carvings of basketballs, flowers, smiley faces, and hearts. Donald sat down, allowing the three of us to do the same. I sat on the corner of the bed, closest to Donald and the desk, while Peter and Father Powell sat in two chairs in the corner of the room.

"Did you do all these carvings?" I asked him as I perused the desk. He nodded. I pointed to a heart with the letters "AD" carved in the middle of it. "Is this for your grandmother?"

Donald nodded again. "Ammey. Yeah, that's Ammey."

"Amy Devonshire," Father Powell clarified.

Peter approached the desk and examined the carvings. "What about this one? Who is 'M'?"

The boy leaned away from Peter, bit his lip, and blinked his eyes.

Father Powell patted Peter's leg. "Please sit down, Father Peter."

Peter returned to his chair and Donald relaxed a bit. He played with his ball again, gingerly tapping it back and forth between his hands.

"So Donald," I began, "do you enjoy working at Our Lady of the Sea?"

"Must keep her floors clean," he replied. "Dirty floors make fo' dirty shoes."

"That couldn't be truer," I agreed. "It sounds like you spend a lot of time at the church, keeping those floors and pews clean. Father Powell tells us you're a hard worker."

Donald did not answer this time. He swayed back and forth in his seat, playing with the basketball. He clung to the orange ball and constantly patted the scaly rubber.

Peter decided to take his chance at asking a question. "When you say keep 'her' floors clean, do you mean the statue, the statue at the front of the church?"

Donald picked at the ball.

"Listen to them, Donald," Father Powell insisted. "Answer their questions. I know you can hear them."

"I keep . . . I keep her floors clean," Donald finally said. I realized we may not get a better answer on this particular question and moved the discussion forward.

"We understand the statue told you she would warm the earth, but you don't feel the heat inside the church, do you?" Donald shook his head. "Why is that?"

"Her home feel like it always do."

"But why is it that *you* don't feel the heat?" Peter persisted from the other side of the room. I was surprised to see him taking interest in the situation after his distant behavior all morning.

Donald turned to Father Powell and spoke in a loud, erratic tone. "Her home feel like it always do, Fader Powell. Like it always do. Like it always do. Like it always—"

"Okay, Donald," Father Powell interrupted. "Okay. Calm down."

Father Powell glanced at us. It was becoming more and more clear why he hadn't told us about this boy at first. Still, I pressed on. "What about when the statue talked to you about the shepherd? What did she say about this shepherd of the church?"

"She say we have a visitor to her home soon, real soon. She say, she say, she say she warm the earth."

"That's what we heard," I said. "But did she say anything else? Did she say who this visitor was, or *why* she was warming the earth?"

Donald only repeated everything he had just said, word for word. Peter let out a powerful sigh and leaned over to me. "This is going nowhere. Let's get out of here."

I ignored Peter. "Donald, Father Powell told us the statue would stop giving off heat when 'it' passes."

"Uh-huh. Dat's what she say. When it come to pass."

"When *what* comes to pass?" I asked. "What will happen?"

"She knows," was all he said.

"But we need to know," I pleaded. "We need to know if anything will happen, and if we can prevent anyone from getting hurt."

Donald shook his head and laughed. "No, no. She knows. We not supposed to see yet. Why you think you need ta' know when she knows for you?"

No matter what I asked, Donald didn't give us any helpful information, and in fact he kept turning the conversation back to the Celtics. I tried my best not to get frustrated with him, but that proved difficult. I wanted so badly for him to say something that cleared up this whole matter. I didn't know what I expected, but I expected more than what I was getting.

In the midst of Donald telling us about the Celtics upcoming season, Peter interrupted him with another question, one I hadn't planned on asking.

"Where are your parents, Donald?"

Donald paused and looked to Father Powell.

"Do you know where your parents are?" Peter asked again. "Why don't you live with them?"

"Mommy and Daddy gone."

"They didn't want you?"

"Peter," I grunted under my breath, "cut it out."

"Ammey wants me," Donald answered.

"But your parents didn't?" Peter asked, ignoring my fierce stare. "Why didn't they want you?"

Donald shrugged. "Ammey's my favorite. She love me fine, and . . . and, and make me happy. I told you, Mister, about the message. She knows. Why you need ta' know when she knows for you?"

"Who knows?" I asked. "Your grandmother? Did you tell your grandmother more than you're telling us?"

Donald didn't answer. He stared directly at Peter, so much that Peter had to look away.

"Why his eyes so sad, Fader Powell?"

Father Powell and I looked back and forth between one another. "What was that, Donald?" he asked.

"Why this man's eyes so sad?"

Donald pointed to Peter, but then seemed to lose interest in his own question. He put his basketball on the ground and fidgeted with his fingers, as if he were trying to crack his knuckles.

"Why do you think his eyes look sad?" Father Powell finally asked.

"Cause they look sad, sad like when my puppy can't play. Puppies need to play, Fader Powell."

Father Powell forced out a nervous chuckle. "Donald's dog is about ten years old, but he'll always be a puppy."

It was apparent that I had lost all control of the situation. Before I could get us back on track, Peter stood up.

"This isn't doing any good. We didn't come here to talk about the Celtics and puppies. I think it's time we headed back to Worcester." I didn't get up from my chair, still trying to make sense of everything. "Paul," Peter said even louder than before, "don't you think it's time we leave?"

Struggling for words, I agreed. "Sure. Sure, I suppose we've tried everything we could." I stood up and held out my hand. "It was nice to meet you, Donald." He looked at my hand like I had a disease. "We have Father Powell's phone number so we'll be in touch about trying to get you to a Celtics game."

"Oh, thank you," Donald said, now grabbing my hand with both of his and shaking it with all his power.

We watched from the hallway as Father Powell said good-bye to Donald, making him promise he would not go back to the church today. Donald said he wouldn't but didn't seem to be paying attention. He had begun to flip through a stack of baseball cards piled on his desk.

A few moments later, Father Powell joined us in the hall-way. "I'm sorry this meeting wasn't more beneficial. It may be best to keep everything about Donald between us. If he can't be more specific or clear about what the statue is telling him, I'm not sure we should involve him in all this. It may be too overwhelming for him, and I don't see further questioning providing any answers."

"I agree," Peter said. "We'll return to Worcester and tell Fr. Chase what we've seen, minus anything about Donald. From there, it'll be in his hands to relay all this to the Bishops. We've done everything we can do here."

I didn't know what I thought, but I nodded without realizing it.

"Well, I'll be glad to take you to Mrs. O'Day's. She'll be able to help get you some train tickets back to Boston. I think we should—"

"There's anoder lady," Donald shouted from his room. He didn't look up at us, but only sat there, slightly wiggling his head as he looked at his baseball cards. Father Powell slowly walked back into Donald's bedroom.

"What did you say, Donald?"

Donald looked up at the ceiling. "There be's anoder lady a' the sea, Fader Powell."

"What do you mean, 'another lady'?"

Donald stood up and approached Father Powell as Peter and I returned to the bedroom. Donald rocked back and forth on his heels and stared down at the shag carpet. Placing his hands around Father Powell's left arm, Donald whispered into his ear. *"There be anoder, anoder sea lady that warmin' the earth. You know this, Fader Powell?"*

Father Powell backed up to look Donald in the eyes. "Another lady? You mean there's another statue giving off heat?"

"Yeah," Donald answered in another whisper. *"Yeah. Yeah."* He gently swiped at Father Powell's shoulder, removing some lint, then went back to the baseball cards on his desk.

"Where is this statue?" I asked from behind Father Powell.

Donald didn't answer. He sat in his chair and mumbled something under his breath.

"Donald?" Father Powell said.

"Yeah, Fader Powell?"

"Where is this other statue you're talking about?"

"Yeah, there be's anoder warm lady, Fader Powell. She in this same sea as here in my home."

"But where exactly?" I asked. "Is it in your church here in Jamestown?"

"No, no," Donald answered with a playful giggle that actually frightened me. "Not here . . . anoder lady, different lady a' the sea. She warmin' the eart' too, Fader Powell. Not just our lady of the sea. Anoder lady."

Father Powell, Peter and I looked back and forth between one another, speechless.

13

I GOT in late from Atlanta and dragged myself to bed. I had only been gone for a couple days but it seemed I was away from Edisto for months. As I lay there under my cool, white sheets, I glanced over to the disposable camera resting on my bedside table, thinking of Sr. Marie. I couldn't wait to show Walt the pictures I had taken of her and the orphanage grounds in Sandy Springs.

But at the precise moment a bolt of lightning flashed outside, a horrible thought ripped its way across my mind. I had told Walt I was visiting my nephew. How would he react when I told him the truth? I was sure he'd be hurt that I had lied to him, but considering he usually didn't like people meddling in his affairs, he might be enraged that I had tried to track down his son without his permission. I was only trying to help, but I'd gone about it in the wrong way. I should have been honest with him.

Unable to sleep, I looked out my window for nearly an hour, watching as the clouds rolled atop the ocean and the lightning tore up the sky. It sounded as if the gods were shooting cannon balls at one another as the thunder boomed every so often above me. By the time I climbed back in bed, I had decided not to tell Walt where I'd been that weekend. I was taking the cowardly way out.

A week later I got the pictures developed. I sat in the parking lot of the photo store and flipped through the ten or so snapshots I had taken. The last one of Sr. Marie tugged on my conscience so much I couldn't ignore it. I drove home slower than usual, trying to anticipate how I would go about this conversation. When I pulled in my driveway, I was surprised to see Walt unloading a new corduroy chair from his truck. It looked to be one of those lazy-boys, the kind with a movable leg rest and big arm pads.

After parking, I ran over to his yard. "Are you crazy?" I yelled. "You can't move that thing by yourself!"

Walt had dragged it to his front steps before he stopped for a breather. Sam sat on the porch panting as he supervised. "You okay?" I asked, putting my hand on his back.

"I'm fine," he said between heavy breaths, "just give me a sec."

"Why don't you sit down," I suggested. "You got a chair right here for gosh sakes." Walt slumped into the chair. "You don't seem like one to get new furniture, Walt. What made you purchase this thing?"

After a few more deep breaths he could answer. "I saw this in a store this past weekend and couldn't resist after I sat down in it. It's going to be my new nap chair."

"That's all well and good, but you're 'bout to let it kill you, trying to bring it in by yourself like this."

"You may be right. If I was a normal man in good health I might be able to do it, but I got this weak lung thing that I've had since I was a young man, and it ain't improved any since I became an old man. You mind giving me a hand?"

"Course not. I got something I want to talk to you about anyway."

We lifted the chair up his front steps and into his den. He changed his mind a few times on where he wanted it, but I gritted my teeth and bore it patiently. I wasn't looking forward to telling Walt what I had to tell him, but waiting to tell him was even worse. Finally, he had a spot that pleased him in the corner of the room, by a window overlooking the beach. Before he could take a seat in his new chair, the buzzer from his dryer went off. "Oh, let me get those clothes so I can fold 'em while we visit."

I sighed; yet another delay that would eat away at my insides. To settle myself I looked around Walt's den. He had a few old war medals scattered on a large credenza and several black and white pictures of his friends from the service. Behind those I saw a picture of Olivia, and next to that one I saw a photo of Walt and myself, taken the day we went out fishing on my friend's boat. I had forgotten about giving him a copy of this picture. I smiled at seeing it placed alongside Olivia and Walt's war buddies; I was in good company. There was only one picture on the table I was unsure of. It was of a little girl with brown complexion and dark, scraggly hair. She was alone, leaning up against the wall of a bamboo hut with somber eyes meeting the camera lens. It was a strange picture compared to all the others; one I had never noticed before.

Walt came back into the den with a pile of warm, wrinkled clothes. They were in bad need of an iron, but I knew he wouldn't bother.

"Say, Walt, who is this little girl?"

He dropped the clothes onto his sagging sofa and glanced at the picture. "Oh, that's a little girl from Costa Rica I sponsor through my church. It's one of those deals where you send a few dollars each month and a letter every now and again. I don't know how much help it actually is, but I like doing it, and every once in a while I'll get a letter back from her, translated of course by someone else. I started it about a year ago; didn't I tell you?"

"Don't think you did, though it wouldn't be the first time I forgot something."

Walt went back across the room, plopped himself down on his new chair, and reached over to his couch to retrieve a shirt to fold. "All right, Buck, what's on your mind?"

"Well," I began, except that was all I had. Everything I had planned on the way over slipped through my ears like a breeze flying through an open window. In desperation, I pulled the pictures from my pocket. "Maybe you should take a look at these photos."

Walt eyed me as he took the pictures. He pulled them out of the white sleeve and flipped through them one-by-one. When he got to the one with Sister Marie in it, he laughed. "What the hell are these pictures of? And since when did you start carrying-on with nuns?"

"Those are pictures of a children's home in Sandy Springs, Georgia, right outside Atlanta."

"A children's home?"

"That's right. But it used to be an orphanage." Walt's expression dropped. I took a deep breath. "I didn't go visit my nephew last week."

After a short pause, he said, "Where'd you go, then? Did you go to this place?"

"I feel bad about lying, but I knew you wouldn't have let me go if I told the truth."

"What the heck are you talkin' about?"

I looked down to the floor. "I went over to Aiken. I tried to track down your boy, Walt."

"You did what?" Walt leaned forward in his chair.

"Just hear me out, now. I got some stuff I want to tell you."

"You lied to me."

"I know, but I meant well."

"I told you; I tried over twenty years ago. It was pointless! I didn't find anything, and I bet you didn't either."

"You're right, mostly. There wasn't much I could do without a name for the boy, and I realize that now. But when I left last Wednesday I had a notion that I could stumble onto something."

Walt stood up and strode into his kitchen. He grabbed a cup and filled it with water from the faucet. After he took a big gulp of water he returned to the den and sat down.

"What do you mean I was 'mostly' right?"

"That's what I wanted to talk with you about, if you'll just listen. I didn't find your boy; let me start by making that clear. And I didn't find any definite information on where he could have been sent. But I spoke with someone at the Aiken hospital and learned something that you may not have known."

"And what might that be?" I could tell his anger was turning into curiosity.

"First, they sent me away for the day and directed me

toward the Home for Little Angels, the place you told me about. Like you said, they weren't too helpful there. But when I returned to the hospital the next day, a social worker there said during a small period in the nineteen fifties they were allowed to send a lot of the kids to this orphanage outside Atlanta, because of overcrowding, or, or something like that. The man there said he wouldn't have been surprised if your boy was sent there since the rules weren't as strict back then about keeping kids within the state. So I drove on down."

Walt shook his head and laughed sarcastically, but I could tell this piece of information came as a surprise to him. "You sure are dumb to do all this," he said. "What'd you think you'd find down there?"

"You want me to continue or not?"

"Go on."

"When I got there, I got directions to the suburb where the children's home was, in Sandy Springs. It's a real nice town, kind of has that small town feel like Edisto does even though it's so close to the big city. But anyway, I eventually found this place back in the woods, and man I tell you, Walt, it was so pretty back in there . . . real nice landscape and lots of fine buildings. Just look at the photos." I stopped while he took another look at the pictures. "That woman there is named Sister Marie Joseph," I went on. "I spoke with her for a while. She told me that the home used to serve as an orphanage, but a while back it got turned into a home for kids from abusive households and local Atlanta kids whose families have trouble keeping after them. Sister Marie's been there since the fifties, when it was still an orphanage, so she would've been around when your boy was there. *If* he was there, that is. She's a real nice woman, sharp as a whip but as sweet as can be. She and the other nuns tutor the children, take them to church, let them play on a real nice playground, and the ones who sleep there get tucked into bed every night. It couldn't be a better place to grow up, Walt. I could tell those nuns treat the kids like their own kin."

Without looking up from the pictures, he said, "What is this supposed to do for me?"

I shrugged. "I don't know. I just figured it might give you some peace of mind to know that your boy may have grown up *there* instead of that place in Aiken. I know it's a long shot, but think how much better his life could've been if he got sent to Atlanta and lived with those nuns. They're Catholic, just like you. Wouldn't that make you feel better to know he was raised there?"

"This is just a stupid fantasy," Walt grunted.

"Now I don't know why you gotta' go and say that. You don't know if—"

"What good is it to believe something like this?" he interrupted. "Every time I picture my son, I see a face filled with anger towards me, and I know that's anger I deserve. A couple pictures of a nice orphanage where he may or may not have lived, isn't going to change what happened. I know you want to believe my son has lived a good life, maybe even at this place. But it really doesn't matter if he did have a good life, because it still wouldn't be the life he was supposed to have. That thought is going to pain me no matter what you do, Buck. You shouldn't have lied to me, and you shouldn't have done this. You've only made me wonder even more about what could have been. Now please, I'd like you to leave."

"Come on, Walt."

"Leave, now. You're not welcome here. And take your pictures with you."

He stuffed them down in the white sleeve and tried to hand them to me, but I wouldn't take them. I stood up and walked toward the door. The floorboards creaked below my slow and heavy footsteps, echoing throughout the silent house.

"Ya' know," I said as I opened his back door. "I understand you're a church farin' man and all, but you need to learn something about forgiveness. Anger towards yourself is the same as anger towards your neighbor. I don't know much, but I know if God believes you truly regret something in your heart, he forgives you for it. Nothing I did last week will change your past and I understand that just the same as you, but at some point you got to accept life and move on with it."

He still wouldn't look at me or respond, so I left and let the screen door close behind me. Instead of going back to my house, I walked onto the beach and took off my shoes. I did my best to let the late afternoon sunshine and soft sand relax me as I walked across the empty coast. I picked up a few sea shells along the way and chucked them against the tumbling waves, trying to force my frustration into the sea.

I returned to my home as dusk fell. But before I could make it into my backyard, the sight of Walt moving inside his house caught my attention. I stood still, knowing I shouldn't be this nosey, but too curious to look away. He approached his mantle above the fireplace with a picture in his hands, looked down at it for several seconds, then grabbed a frame from the mantle and placed the picture inside.

14

NO MATTER how hard we tried to get things out of him, Donald would not divulge any more information about a second statue. As Father Powell drove us back to Mrs. O'Day's house, we discussed the boy's latest claim. Father Powell assured us this was the first he had heard of a second statue from Donald. We wondered how long the boy had known about this, and whether or not it could be true. Father Powell remained certain that Donald was telling the truth because all his other claims about the statue seemed to be accurate. Peter had his doubts and gave the impression he was through chasing such ambiguous leads.

Peter and I considered going back to the church in Jamestown one last time, but I could tell Peter had no desire to do so. I didn't want to put him on edge any more than he already was, so I agreed to head back to Worcester. We told Father Powell we would speak with Father Chase about what we had seen, and from there it would be his decision on how to proceed. We knew Father Chase would consult with the Bishops and they would probably inform the Cardinal in Boston of the whole matter.

When it came to the issue of informing others about what Donald had said, we disagreed once again. Peter wanted to leave Donald out of it all together, telling no one outside the three of us about him. Peter argued that the validity of this phenomenon would never be justified if Donald were brought into it. I wasn't sure if that was the *real* reason Peter didn't want to divulge anything about Donald, but it was a good point. Father Powell saw things both ways, in that he wanted the Church to consider every aspect of the situation, but he didn't want any pressure or excessive attention directed toward Donald. Father Powell worried for the boy, knowing he would not do well when this story reached the national spotlight.

I found myself being quite adamant in at least telling Father Chase about Donald. If he felt Donald and his conversations with the statue should be left alone, I would go along with that decision. By the same token, if Father Chase found Donald to be an integral part of explaining this happening, I couldn't disagree.

I thought the matter was settled until we reached the train station. We had just said goodbye to Mrs. O'Day and were waiting patiently on a bench in the main hall of the station for our departing train.

"The only reason I'm agreeing to divulge anything about Donald is because Father Chase is a good man," Peter said, "and it doesn't feel right to keep things from him. But just imagine if one of the national media outlets gets wind of this situation. They will pounce on the Church and make us look like a bunch of nuts; then they'll start in on Donald."

"Why do you care what people think of the Catholic Church? You said you were leaving when we got back."

He ignored my attempt to discuss his future.

"I'm just being realistic here. The rest of the world already thinks we're bordering on idolatry for putting statues in our churches, and most believe we worship Mary. Now we're going to tell them that we believe she's speaking through a statue to a mentally challenged boy? Do you think that will go over well?"

"I'm not concerned with how it will go over; I'm concerned for the truth. I can't help that some people are offended by the statues in our churches, but then put up manger scenes at Christmastime and fail to see the similarity there. They know they aren't idolizing those figurines resting on their mantel, just like we aren't idolizing the statues in our churches. We need things like that present to bring our hearts and minds back to God when our thoughts wander to trivial, earthly matters. And I know we're not worshipping Mary; you do as well, Peter. You shouldn't worry about what people think and say, you should worry about what you believe. We honor Mary, just as Jesus did, from the time he began his ministry and preformed his first miracle in Cana at her request, to some of his last words on the cross when he said to John, 'Behold, your mother.' The basic premise of Christianity is to emulate Christ in *every* way, so we treat Mary with the same respect that he did. I wish others would see things that way and not misunderstand her role within the Church, but for the most part that's out of my control. We need to focus on the truth of what's happening here, not how the rest of the world will view this."

"But it just *had* to be a statue of Mary, didn't it? It couldn't have at least been a statue of Jesus radiating heat to help make this a little easier on us?"

"Peter, the rest of the world may not view Mary in the light we do, but they know God used her to bring his son into the world. Mary brought Jesus to all the nations, just like any Christian disciple who journeys across the globe preaching in Christ's name. In this way, she was the first ever missionary. At that wedding in Cana she told the servants, 'Do whatever he tells you.' That wasn't a message directed solely at those servants; it was a message to all of us, from the very mouth of Christ's own mother. She wasn't asking for our worship and we don't give it to her. She was asking us to follow her son. This wouldn't be the first time God has used Mary to bring people closer to Christ. We shouldn't be surprised that it is a statue of *her* doing this."

"I just . . . look, all we should really do is remove the statue from the church. Then those people can get their lives back to normal and we can all move on."

"Perhaps we should remove the statue, but we shouldn't move on until we've made sense of this."

"And how do you figure on making any sense of this mess?"

"We both know there is no guidebook or list of rules to follow when things like this happen. All we can do is pray, trust our gut instincts and follow the evidence laid before us."

"Evidence? Tell me you don't call Donald's claims evidence?"

A voice boomed over the speakers of the station, inform-ing the passengers of the next departing train. It wasn't announcing the one we were waiting to board, but the noise sliced through our dispute and deflated me. I didn't have the energy to argue anymore. I headed to a vending machine tucked away in the corner of the main hall, placed a couple coins in the slot, and listened as the can tumbled to the bottom of the machine. I gulped down the fuzzy liquid, hoping the caffeine would perk my energy.

After a few minutes spent standing alone, I heard them finally call our train. I glanced over to where Peter had been sitting, but his seat was empty.

15

AFTER FOUR days of not speaking to Walt, I paused in the novel I was reading to stare out my side window at the drizzling rain, just in time to see him hurrying toward my house. He didn't knock after he had climbed the back steps. Instead, he slid a white envelope under the crack beneath my door, then jogged back to his own house, doing his best to avoid the lazy rain.

I didn't get up at first. I stayed put in my blue-cloth chair and proceeded to read the novel in my lap, determined to reach the end of the chapter before retrieving the envelope.

I reached the end of that chapter, glanced at the envelope, then continued to the next chapter. Plain fear kept me from putting the book down through the course of three more chapters. I was kidding myself if I thought I was paying attention to the story. My gaze slid over some pages three times before I'd actually read a word. After an hour I got up and made some dinner, still leaving the envelope sitting on the floor. It stared at me like a sad puppy wanting attention as I fried a grilled cheese on my stove.

At ten o'clock, with the sun long set and the rain journeyed down the coast, I snatched it off the floor and walked outside to my back porch, planting myself in a rocker. The night sky was as black as a witch's cauldron, with not a star in sight or a moon to speak of. I pulled out the note and unfolded it, the paper popping like my old bones as I rose from bed each morning. I read Walt's letter using the glow from the window over my shoulder:

Dear Buck,

I'm sorry for how I jumped on you last week. Passing time can be the best prescription for understanding a difficult matter, and I see now that you only meant well. I hate that you lied to me about where you went, but I reckon I can forgive a white lie.

When I tried to find my son so many years ago, I was told by the authorities that my boy would've grown up in that orphanage, and that he would've stayed there until a family had claimed him, which sometimes took years. So I went about my life thinking my own flesh and blood spent his years living in a run-down, group home, being raised by people who didn't know about the life me and the boy's mother wanted for our son. But I suppose I can't hold those people responsible for that.

That day I walked out of that hospital, I pushed my boy away forever. But no day was worse than when I came back ten years later and saw the place where he would have grown up. It made the reality of my decision sink into my bones, and that has weighed me down since then.

But after you left last week, I stared at the picture of that nun, Sister Marie. You told me she was a
kind lady, and that she and the other nuns took care
of the children as if they were their own. You told
me this home was as nice a place to grow up as any
place could be. I don't know if my son spent any time
at that home, but Sister Marie's picture is sitting on
my mantle now. She's not a stranger somehow, and
that comforts me for reasons I can't explain.

I am indebted to you for the efforts you made
in trying to reconcile my sins. I won't forget what
you've done.

Sincerely,
Walt.

P.S. I'd like you to be on the beach tomorrow when
I play. I want to introduce you to Olivia.

I folded up the letter, placed it in my shirt pocket and let
the ocean's waves put me to sleep.

When I felt a soft glow on my face, it was clear a new
day had arrived. I walked out on the beach through the salty,
morning mist. Just as I arrived on the cold sand, I heard Walt's
screen door slam. He came my way, carrying his violin and a
chair. Sam galloped toward me on excited paws, surprised to
see a visitor for their morning ritual.

It was clear Walt and I would not say a word to one
another. As he set himself up to play, I sat down on the sand
next to him and looked out over the sea. The sun rose slowly

from the watery horizon, sprinkling the clouds with morning's first light. Sam curled up next to me and took his place in the scene, lying in such a way that seemed to say this was *his* beach. I considered how Walt had done this every morning for the last thirty some years, giving meaning to each day. Like most of mankind, I had managed to let time pass without much thought given to something beyond this world. I was jealous of Walt for experiencing these unique moments, but then I realized it was his tragedies that brought about the meaning he'd found, and I wondered if I should be jealous at all.

My thoughts came to a halt when the music began to rise from beside me. I wasn't sure what piece Walt played, but I knew it was played to perfection. He grazed the strings in such a way that made the skies part and open us up to the heavens above. The sea gulls no longer needed wind to glide through the air; Walt's song carried them wherever they needed to go. I looked upwards and closed my eyes, letting the chills tickle my skin.

I met Walt's wife that morning. His music somehow served as a conversation between Olivia and me, and in only a matter of minutes, we'd become close friends.

The song ended and gave way to the sounds of the beach. The crashing waves returned, the sea gulls squawked once again, and the morning wind whistled as it always did. Walt and I both stood up and shook hands. Still, neither of us spoke a word. We returned to our homes and knew we would never do that again. That was Walt's ritual; I was simply a one-time visitor.

That morning helped us both a great deal. He got over the lie I had told, and I left his past where it needed to be left.

Walt seemed to have finally accepted his sins and would do his best to move on, and I was happy for that. All I wanted was to live out my days in peace, with my friend and neighbor by my side.

But it wasn't long before something else shook our uneventful days; something that would change our lives, and change the way I viewed the world forever.

16

I HURRIED back to where I had been sitting with Peter. His bags were gone but mine remained. I grabbed them and searched the station frantically until I heard the final call for our train. Not knowing what to do, I headed for the train and boarded it. Much to my relief, but also anger, Peter was seated in the first cart, staring out the window.

"What was that about?" I asked, taking the seat next to him.

"What?"

"You left me. I didn't know you had boarded."

"Sorry."

That was all Peter managed to say the whole way back to Worcester. When we arrived on our familiar campus, we tried to set up a time to see Father Chase, but he was tied up for the remainder of the evening, pushing our meeting until the following morning. That night, Peter departed to his bedroom early without eating dinner, but I had something I needed to do before speaking with Father Chase.

I walked across campus about eight in the evening. Most of the students had retired to their dorm rooms, but a few were outside enjoying a cigarette. I walked into the library on the south side of the grounds and was met by the security guard sitting at the front desk, an elderly man everyone called Ace for reasons unknown to me. After exchanging a brief greeting with Ace, I departed to the back of the library. Only a few students were there, letting me concentrate on what I wanted to do. I sat down at an empty desk and went over the notes I had taken from our weekend trip. I heard Donald's words echoing in my mind. *Anoder lady. Anoder lady warmin' the eart'.* On the train ride home, I had considered that perhaps Donald was telling us to look for another church that went by the name, "Our Lady of the Sea." But as I thought about all the Catholic churches in America that could be, or the world, for that matter, I became overwhelmed. The task of finding all those churches and their locations seemed unlikely, or would at least take months of research.

I needed coffee. I walked back to the front desk where Ace sat reading a magazine. I filled a styrofoam cup to the brim and decided to take a break from my investigation and talk with him about something trivial, something that didn't require me to think. But in an instant, Ace had sparked my mind back to the statues.

"What did you just say?" I asked.

"I said my brother caught a small shark last weekend."

"No, before that. Where did you say he was?"

"He was deep sea fishing, out in the Atlantic."

I smiled. "Ace, you're a genius!"

"Now there's something I've never been called," the old man joked.

I laughed and ran back to my desk, trying to keep my arm

steady so I wouldn't spill the coffee. I suddenly felt as if Donald was sitting next to me in the library; I could hear his message that clearly. *She in this same sea as here in my home.* Sitting back down, I devised a plan for how to locate all the churches on the eastern seaboard named Our Lady of the Sea.

For the next three hours I flipped through stacks of books, Catholic magazines and diocese newsletters; I sifted through old periodicals; I made phone calls to Bishops up and down the east coast asking them about the churches in their dioceses, catching the wrath of some because of the late hour. When I couldn't reach a Bishop, I called priests and even friends and family living in the targeted areas, imploring them to check their local phone books for the information I sought. It was hard to gauge the accuracy of my research, but when it was all said and done, I had only found four other churches on the east coast that shared a name with the Rhode Island church. I spent another hour doing research on the four other parishes, locating them on maps Ace retrieved for me from a library closet. When I finally stopped to look at the time, I saw it was long past midnight. I lugged my tired body back to my room, but slept little. I tossed and turned as I thought about our meeting with Father Chase. I had to handle the situation delicately, and before I went in, I knew I needed to make a phone call and ask for a favor from my brother back in Michigan.

The next morning I awoke early, making a few more phone calls to confirm what I had discovered the night before. I didn't even see Peter until we met each other in Father Chase's office after lunch.

I did most of the talking, while Peter merely stared straight ahead. Father Chase asked questions as he listened to my report with an attentive ear. When the discussion turned to Donald, he seemed frightened by what we told him. He glanced at Peter when I told him about the message from the statue, about a shepherd made of the rock, but he didn't address the message specifically when I finished my report.

"This is pretty daunting to hear," Father Chase began. "I don't know what I expected you to find, but I didn't expect this. The challenged boy being such a big part of this means we have to be even more sensitive in how we handle it. It's hard to put a lot of stock in these messages he supposedly hears, but what you say about him not being affected by the heat, that's reason to take notice of him. I like your suggestion, Peter, of having the statue removed from the church, perhaps so it can be studied, but also so the people of the town can get their lives back to normal. I'll suggest this to the Bishops, but from there it's out of my hands. At some point this story will get out, but for now, we still need to keep this secretive until we know more. This will be easier for everyone involved if we can keep the reporters and cameras away for a few more days, or at least until a more stringent investigation can be done."

"And what about the possibility of a second statue?" I asked.

Father Chase shrugged his shoulders. "I'm as curious about that as you are, Paul, but what can we do? If this boy didn't give you any specific information, we can't go any further with this. If there is another heated statue, that parish may be keeping quiet as well. Maybe there's another set of priests having a meeting like this somewhere else in the world, but how could we possibly know that?"

"I actually did some work last night, and I have a theory."
I could feel Peter's eyes on me.

"Okay, what do you have, Paul?"

"Well, Donald said there was another, 'lady of the sea warming the earth.' I took that to mean another statue in another church called, 'Our Lady of the Sea.' So I went to the library last night and did some research, making dozens of phone calls. I discovered that, as near as I could tell, there are only four churches by this name on the east coast, outside of the one we visited in Rhode Island."

"What does the east coast have to do with it?" Peter asked.

"Donald said this other lady was, 'in this same sea as the one in my home,'" I answered, glancing at my notes. "I know that doesn't make perfect sense, but I think that means the Atlantic Ocean. His hometown and church are right on the water, so maybe this other statue is also located somewhere near the Atlantic Ocean."

Peter huffed under his breath from the seat next to me, but I ignored him.

"I'm still listening," Father Chase assured me, although I could tell he was skeptical.

I looked down at my notes again. "After calling several Bishops, priests, and some friends and family, looking through old articles and books, and reviewing countless maps, I found that the four other churches are in Maine, South Carolina, and there are two in Florida. The one in Maine is almost ten miles inland, as is the one in Miami. But one church near Jacksonville seems to be right on the coast, as does the one in South Carolina. They are literally directly on the water, just like the one in Rhode Island. I think we should look into these two

churches and see if anything unusual is happening. If we discover another heated statue, we'll know for sure that Donald
is telling the truth, and we'll be a step closer to understanding
this miracle."

"Don't forget the statue is keeping people away from
church," Peter interjected, "and terrifying people. Doesn't
something good have to happen for it to be considered a
miracle?"

"That's not necessarily true," Father Chase answered.
"Certain events throughout history may not have served a
clear purpose, but they can give us signs that there is something beyond this world. Think about Fatima and the day the
sun danced; that was terribly frightening for those people,
but as we look back on it we see the miracle in its entirety.
You should know better, Peter." He stared at Peter for several seconds but Peter didn't respond. "Look," Father Chase
said turning his focus back to me, "I love the passion you're
showing in pursuing this, but we still don't know anything for
certain, and we don't have the resources to send you two on a
wild goose chase. If you want to make some phone calls and try
to gather more concrete evidence of a second statue, then you
have my permission. But otherwise, we'll have to wait and see
what develops."

"I think we need to do more than that. I've taken care
of the resources so that it won't cost the school or diocese any
money to send Peter and me down south."

"How is that?" Father Chase asked.

"I figured we didn't have the funds for another trip, so I
called my brother in Michigan this morning and asked if he
would make a donation. I didn't tell him what was going on

with the statue, but he trusts me and has agreed to pay whatever it takes to get us where we need to go: plane tickets, car rentals, hotels, food, and anything else we need."

"Are you sure he can afford to do that?"

"Absolutely. He's a successful lawyer and his wife has a great job as well."

"But why travel all over the country and spend his money? Why wouldn't a few phone calls work?"

This was an argument I was expecting to hear, whether from Father Chase or Peter, and technically, I didn't have an answer. The truth was that I felt I needed to make sure Peter saw this mission through to the end. I knew if I took the lead in the investigation by myself, remaining here at our campus and only making phone calls, Peter would simply fade away and possibly leave us for good. But if he was *forced* to take another trip, I felt I might have more time to speak with him and have his full attention. Most importantly, I prayed that if we journeyed down south Peter would find something which renewed his faith. I knew all this phenomenon with the statues had something to do with him; I was sure of it, even if Peter was resisting it.

But I couldn't explain all this to Father Chase because he was unaware of all that was happening to Peter.

I took a deep breath. "I don't know if I can explain it, sir. I just think Peter and I need to visit these towns. I feel a call to see this through. We can learn so much more by seeing these churches with our own eyes and speaking with the people involved. Think about if we had just *called* Jamestown and didn't actually go there; we would have probably never known about Donald and his messages. I just feel we'll be placing ourselves in a better position to understand this if we're willing to put in the extra effort."

Father Chase took his turn at taking a deep breath as he ran his hand through his thinning, weathered hair. I glanced over at Peter, who stared at me sullenly. I knew he wanted to move on from what we had seen in Rhode Island, but I wouldn't let him forget. Not yet.

"I respect your desire to see this through," Father Chase said. "And I understand your sentiments in feeling a call to follow through on this. Sometimes we get feelings we can't explain, and usually those are the feelings we should pay the most attention to. I suppose I have no excuse to keep you from going if it won't cost us anything. Where exactly are these towns?"

"One is in St. Augustine, Florida, just south of Jacksonville, and the other is in Edisto Island, South Carolina. Both these churches are built right on the coast and are only about five hours apart. I figure we can fly into Florida and rent a car. From there, we could—"

"Now wait a minute," Peter interrupted. "You can't be serious about sending us halfway across the country on a whim like this, can you, Father Chase?"

"Why are you so skeptical?" I asked him, not giving Father Chase a chance to answer. "Donald said the statue would warm the earth, and she did. Why shouldn't we follow a lead if Donald says there's another statue somewhere?"

"I won't even broach the subject of whether or not Donald could possibly know the truth," Peter replied, "but let's just say he does for argument's sake. How do we know either of these two churches you found could be the right place to go? Maybe Donald was confused about which 'sea' the statue said and it's really on the west coast. Maybe it *is* the Atlantic, but it's in Europe or Africa somewhere. Did you look for churches all over the world that go by Our Lady of the Sea? No, of course you didn't. Maybe in your research you didn't find every church on the east coast called Our Lady of the Sea. What about all the churches called, 'Lady Star of the Sea' or any other similar name? There may be five or ten other churches on the east coast you don't even know about that this supposed second statue could be at. And what if your original assumption is wrong? What if we shouldn't even be looking for churches called Our Lady of the Sea?"

"All that could be true, but I don't think God sent us to Rhode Island by accident, Peter, and I don't think all that has happened since then is an accident either. We need to continue on with this journey and see this through to the end, or we'll regret it for the rest of our lives. I can't . . ."

I stopped my when Peter put his face in his hands.

"Are you all right, Peter?" Father Chase asked, also noticing his discomfort.

Peter kept his face buried in his trembling hands. Father Chase watched, bewildered. I laid my hand and on Peter's shoulder, but he swiped it away. "You're driving me nuts with this," he snapped. "What are you trying to do? Do you think if we go down there and find another heated statue my life will be perfect all of a sudden?"

"Of course not. But why do you want to brush this away like nothing is happening? Forget about Donald for a minute, and forget about your past; I *know* you felt the heat. You can't deny that."

"I don't want anything to do with it, and I don't know why you can't understand that. I'm leaving, Paul. You trying to force the issue only makes me want to leave even more. I told you that would happen the night you caught me leaving and begged me to stay. You just need to let me be, let me leave. You don't understand what I'm going through. You can't see things from my perspective."

"Okay, you two," Father Chase said, rising to his feet. "Someone needs to tell me what's going on." Both Peter and I ignored him, but Father Chase took control. "All right, Paul, why don't you step outside for a minute and let me talk with Peter. But please don't leave."

I stepped outside his office, refusing to look at Peter as I left. The next thirty minutes felt like an eternity. I didn't want to go far but I couldn't sit down, so I paced up and down a nearby marble hallway.

What could I possibly do at this point to alleviate Peter's anguish? Each second that passed without an answer to that question sunk me deeper and deeper into depression. In continuing my pacing, I began a dialog with God.

What is it that you want me to do to help my friend? What are you doing with this statue? If you knew this would distance Peter even more, why are you letting it happen? Why did you let that girl in Costa Rica suffer so much? Why did you let Peter meet her if you knew she would bring back his bitterness? Why are you letting Peter slip away?

Father Chase's secretary, Mrs. Ferris, was an older lady who served as an honorary grandmother figure to everyone at the college. She could tell when something wasn't right. She approached me with a cup of water. "All hard times come to pass, my dear." She gripped my hand and squeezed it tightly. I didn't know what to do except hug her. The smell of her faded, cotton sweater reminded me of simpler times. She held me without speaking. Her secure clutch nearly brought me to tears, but I thanked her and composed myself.

Father Chase's door opened a second later. "Paul," he yelled down the hallway. "Can you come back in here?" My steps toward his door seemed to echo throughout the whole building. When I entered his office, I saw Peter standing in the middle of the room with his hands in his pockets, his head hung toward the Oriental rug draping the hardwood floor.

"Paul," Father Chase began as he put his hand on my shoulder, "Peter has informed me of what's been going on with him for the last few weeks, or years, for that matter. It saddens me, and I wish his feelings toward the life he chose were different." He paused and turned to Peter. "We've had a nice, long discussion about what's buried deep within his heart, and we've talked about his future. I've told him I can't have you going on this trip by yourself, and he knows you only mean well. Peter has agreed to go south with you for a few days. After that, I'm sending him away on sabbatical for at least a few months, maybe even a year. That time away will give him a chance to straighten himself out. But I've told him if his feelings don't change, then he needs to think about ending his vocation. As sad as I will be if Peter leaves us for good, I can't have a priest here who views the world the way he does."

I fought back my emotions as best I could. "I understand. Thank you for agreeing to go with me, Peter."

Peter pursed his lips and nodded. He moved through the

doorway and out of sight down the hall, leaving me and Father Chase alone to wonder what the future held for the Peter Davis we once knew.

17

TIME PASSED slowly for Walt and me in the next year or so. The seasons gave way to one another and we watched as the land cooperated accordingly, retreating in the frigid winter and coming back to life as the weather warmed. The two of us lent each other a hand in the summer of '92 as we fixed up each other's homes. We put a new roof on his place and changed out all the windows in mine. Old men need projects like this. We look for them and find them even when they seem hidden. We kept with our traditions of fishing and playing checkers, and perhaps our favorite of all, avoiding the old ladies down the dirt road.

But one overcast Sunday in September of that year our pattern was thrown off. Usually, the two of us would get together for brunch at a local diner after our separate church services. But Walt never arrived. I was worried at first, especially since he'd been acting strange lately. He seemed distant and distracted, but as usual he wouldn't tell me what was on his mind. When he stood me up for our Sunday brunch it was just another example of his odd behavior. I drove home and saw that Walt wasn't there, furthering my worry. But about thirty minutes later he pulled in his driveway. I watched him through my window and could tell something was up just by the way he was moving.

I walked over and let myself in. Walt sat in his recliner with a cup of ice water in his hand and Sam's head resting on his thigh. "What's goin' on, Walt?"

He looked up at me. "Oh, gosh! I'm sorry, Buck. Something came up at the church and I completely forgot about our meal."

"That's okay," I replied as I took a seat on his couch. "What happened?"

Walt hesitated. "I don't keep much from you, buddy, but I don't even know how to say this." He took a sip of his water. "Would you mind going on a little trip later tonight?"

"Where to?"

"To my church, just across town. I wish I could take you now, but . . . it would just be better if we went at night . . . when no one was there. Why don't you come back over here about nine-thirty and we'll hop in my truck."

"Why don't you tell me what we'll be doing? I'm not one for surprises."

"I understand, but I'm sorry, Buck. I need a little time to think, to figure out how to explain what's on my mind. Can you respect that for now?"

I didn't want to respect that, but I knew I had to. I told Walt I'd see him later in the evening and walked back home, knowing I'd probably look at my watch every five minutes for the rest of the day.

18

THE SUNDAY morning following our meeting with Fr. Chase, Peter and I each packed a small bag and took the commuter rail to Logan International in Boston. Our journey would take us into Jacksonville first with there being no direct flight to the St. Augustine airport. I spent most of our nearly three hour flight in anxious, personal prayer.

When we landed in Jacksonville, we made our way to the car rental counter. We signed some papers, giving us permission to drive the Dodge Stratus my brother had reserved for us. We got a map from the lady behind the counter and headed for the airport exit, where we were met by the sticky, Florida air. Even in September the humidity gripped at our necks and strangled us. We sifted our way through a sea of overly bronzed, elderly people, until we found a shuttle that took us to our rental car.

After mapping out our route, we pulled onto the nearest interstate and headed for St. Augustine. I hadn't driven much over the last fifteen years and it wasn't long before people were honking their horns and waving their fists at my erratic driving. But the rust faded and my skills miraculously returned about ten miles down the road. We headed southwest, a little smoother now, out of Jacksonville and toward the coast. Before we left the city limits we passed a football stadium where the local NFL team played, which sparked an easy-going sports conversation between Peter and me. We found that our friendship returned to normal when we weren't discussing religion, God, or the heated statues, and I was thankful for that despite being sad about the state of Peter's psyche. It was nice for us to drive down the highway with the windows down, the cool wind in our faces and a Tom Petty song playing on the radio.

No matter how much I loved being a priest, it was nice every once in a while to feel like someone with a normal life. I wondered if that was what Peter yearned for, to know a life where every waking second wasn't focused on our duty to God. But I quickly threw the thought out of my mind. I had to find the second statue.

19

I SPENT the rest of Sunday afternoon fixing things up around the house to occupy my mind. My gutter had gotten backed up with leaves, the steps leading up to my front door needed to be replaced with new wood, and a window ledge needed repairing. I enjoyed the work, but the day crawled by like a turtle stuck in tar.

I picked at my dinner and then tried to read a book, until finally, at nine-fifteen, I couldn't stand it anymore. I walked over to Walt's house and found him standing by his front door, knowing I'd be early.

"You ready?"

We climbed in his beat-up Ford and drove through town, hushed by the mood of the night. The quiet streets of Edisto were always slow, but Sunday evenings found a way to put even the street lights to sleep. After the main drag where the shops and restaurants were, we made our way through a patch of large trees covered in moss. I had only been to Walt's church once a few years back for a Fourth of July barbeque, but I'd forgotten the way and was surprised when we pulled off on a side road more dirt than pavement. After a few seconds of weaving through the darkness of the oak trees, we arrived in a gravel lot bordering the coastline. Walt put his truck in park and shut the engine off. We sat quietly for several seconds as he stared straight ahead at the small, stone church. The headlights shinned on it, lighting up the stained glass windows.

"What are we doing here?" I asked, not being able to stand the agonizing quiet anymore.

He cut off his lights, leaving us in the darkness. The noises of the night seeped in through his rolled down windows. "You believe in God, right?" he asked.

"Course I do. You know that."

"But do you *really* believe in Him?" he said turning to me. "Don't just say you do because it's the right thing to say. Stop and think about it for a second."

"What's this about, Walt?"

Walt went back to staring forward at the church. He put his hands on the steering wheel and gripped it tightly.

"Something strange has been happening inside that church," he finally said. "I knew you wouldn't believe me if I told you, that's why I brought you here."

"Are we going inside?" Walt reached in his pocket and brought out a key. "Now wait a minute; you need to tell me what's going on before I go walkin' in there."

Walt took a deep breath. "Two Sundays ago I couldn't help noticing it was a little warm in church, but nothing too out of the ordinary. I really didn't think much of it. But last Sunday was a different story. It must have been ninety degrees in there and my clothes were drippin' with perspiration." He paused.

"Okay."

"Despite it being so uncomfortable, I still didn't pay it any mind. I came home without mentioning it to anyone, chalking it up to bein' old and just having a fever or something."

"Sure, that makes sense."

"Well, I came over here this past Wednesday afternoon to practice for today's service, 'cause we were trying out some new songs for the choir, and again, I felt as hot as ever. But this time a couple other people began to notice the temperature, so I knew I wasn't going crazy. We spoke to our priest, Father Harris, and he acknowledged the heat."

"Maybe your heat pump is goin' haywire." I quickly realized how stupid a comment this was. Walt would not have brought me down here in the middle of the night for something as simple as a busted heat pump. He gave me the courtesy of a polite response.

"No, Father had that looked into on Tuesday by a mechanic in our parish. He said everything seemed to be in order with our heating and air system. He didn't know why it was so hot in there."

"So what's causing the heat, then?"

Walt didn't answer my question directly. "I came here today for Mass, not knowing what to expect. I hoped things were back to normal, but when I showed up everyone was standing outside. Father Harris had locked the doors because it had gotten too hot inside. We all discussed what could be happening for hours. Everyone had a theory, of course, but I think I know the answer."

"And?"

"First let me explain where I sit. The choir is up front, on the left side of the altar. Usually I sit by the wall playing my violin, while the people in front of me do the singing. Well, on the wall above my seat there's a statue of Mary resting on a concrete podium. I never really noticed that I sit right under it, but anyway, on Wednesday, when we were in there practicing, I had this crazy notion it was hotter around this statue than it was everywhere else. So I reached up and touched it when no one was looking, and it burned my hand."

"What're you trying to say, Walt?"

He appeared as if he needed courage to go on. "I swear the heat is coming from that statue, Buck."

"What? How can that be?"

"I know it's crazy, but I'm pretty certain about it. It makes perfect sense. Listen, the first two Sundays I was the only one who felt the heat since I was sitting right under the statue. But now it's getting hotter, so you can feel it all over the church. You'll see when we get in there. The temperature isn't as high in the back of the church, but when you move closer to where the choir sits, to where the statue is, it's almost unbearable."

I stared at him for several seconds, until I leaned back in my seat and rubbed my face. For the first time in my life I felt that one of my friends had gone mad.

"That look you're giving me is why I brought you here. I knew what you'd think. Father Harris told us to keep quiet so the whole town wouldn't think we'd gone crazy, but I had to tell *you*. I trust you more than anybody, Buck. I need you to go inside that church and tell me what you think."

"I don't know. Are we even supposed to be here?"

"No. Father Harris told us to keep away. But I've been coming to this church for over thirty years. I've always had access with this key 'cause I do so much work around here, and we'll only go in and out real quick-like. Please, Buck, I need you to feel what I've felt."

"What if your priest comes?"

"He won't," Walt assured me. "Father Harris lives down the road a good ten minutes in a house the Church owns. Besides, this is why I brought you here at this hour. No one's going to come this way so late in the evenin'."

"Maybe some kind of vent is behind the statue, or there's a leak in the pipes and something's seeping out from the wall where you sit."

"Don't you think we'd see a vent if there was one there? Besides, we told you the heat isn't broken; we aren't even running it right now in this early fall weather. And it sure doesn't smell like any kind of leak in there."

I blinked and tried to think of any other reason to not go inside the church. Nothing came to me.

"Let's get it over with."

The two of us exchanged a look, each of us trying to determine how scared the other was. All he had to do was see my hand shaking as I reached for the door handle to know how terrified I actually was.

20

ST. AUGUSTINE was a smaller city than I had anticipated, easily crossed from one end to the other in about twenty minutes. The area had a Spanish feel, with the architecture, street names, and local monuments dedicated to Spanish settlers. We drove through several neighborhoods on our way to the church and admired the unique houses. Most places in the country you couldn't get away with blue, yellow, and orange colored homes, but the style worked here in this sunny, coastal area of Florida.

We found Our Lady of the Sea in the back of a middle class neighborhood. As expected, it rested about a hundred yards from the crashing Atlantic waves, seen in the distance beyond a busy, two-lane road and a stretch of sandy beach. We approached the front of the stucco church, only to find that the doors were locked.

"What now?" Peter asked.

I didn't answer him as I looked at my watch. It was late afternoon. I figured we must have missed the Sunday morning crowd even though we had taken the earliest flight available.

I walked around the perimeter of the church. It was much

larger than the one in Rhode Island, but I didn't feel that held any merit on finding the statue. Halfway down the side wall, we saw a stone grotto that lassoed our gaze. Two stout palm trees rose up beside it and a small statue of Mary rested inside. I approached the statue as a strong gust of wind blew by, rattling the stiff palm leaves above me. I touched the statue. Looking back to Peter, I shook my head. He seemed relieved.

Around the back of the church, we found an older man trimming the hedges with a mask over his face and grass stains on his pants. "Excuse me!" I yelled over the buzzing of his machine. He quickly turned around, then cut off the weed eater and removed his mask.

"May I help you?"

"I'm sorry to disturb you. My name is Father Paul and this is Father Peter."

He eyed us up and down before deciding he could reveal his name. The trust of strangers was a small benefit of being a priest.

"Alton," he replied. "I'd shake your hand, but . . . ." He held up his dirty hands and chuckled.

"Not a problem," I replied. "We were wondering if you could tell us where the local priest is."

"Father Wade just left to go to the hospital. He's visiting a parishioner."

"Do you know when he'll be back?"

"Can't say for sure. May I help you with something?"

"Do you go here to Our Lady of the Sea, or do you work for the church?"

"No, I go here. I'm retired so I do this voluntarily."

"Okay, well, Peter and I just wanted to speak with someone here at this parish. We're on a mission of sorts."

"I'm listening," Alton said as he placed his trimmer down. I could tell he enjoyed feeling useful. "Is this a charity thing?"

"Not exactly. Do you think you could let us in the church?" I asked, not wanting to explain the reasons behind why we were here. "We need to have a look around."

"No, I only take care of the grounds. I don't have a key."

"I see. When was the last time you were inside the church?"

He eyed me suspiciously. "I went to Mass today; the eight o'clock service."

"And was anything strange going on? Anything out of the ordinary?"

"What the devil do you mean, Father?"

"Was the temperature higher than normal inside, or did any . . ."

I ate my words and couldn't spit them back up. I hadn't planned out how this conversation would go, and my lack of preparation showed. I suppose I had expected to be talking to a priest, but if there was no heated statue here it wouldn't have mattered who I was speaking with. The vacant appearance of Alton's face let me know nothing was happening at this church in St. Augustine.

I hadn't noticed, but Peter had walked back to the car, never having even said a word. I did my best to end the conversation with Alton in a way that didn't scare him or keep him wondering about my sanity. It took a slight bit of fibbing, but I told myself it was better not to tell him too much. I considered waiting for the local priest to return from the hospital to let us inside the church, in case there *was* a heated statue here but perhaps it was only in the first moments of this phenomenon, leaving it unnoticed for now. Father Powell and Mrs. O'Day had said some people didn't notice the heat at first in the Rhode Island church. But something didn't feel right. I was looking for a feeling, a gut instinct, and I didn't have it here.

"That went well," Peter said as I approached the car.

"It shouldn't take long to get to Edisto Island."

21

WALT AND I walked slowly across the gravel lot. When we reached the stairs leading up to the front entrance of the church, I glanced to my right where the ocean waters met the beach. There were thick woods blocking the church from a view of the sea, but you could still see glimmers of moonlight shinning off the water through the brush. We slowly climbed the seven cement steps together. My focus was centered on the large, red doors. As we approached them, I watched as Walt reached into his pocket for the key. When he placed it in the lock and turned the key over, the sound of the deadbolt shifting sides boomed within my ears, silencing the crashing waves, the croaking night frogs, and the rustling of the tree branches in the wind. Everything had gone silent.

Walt opened the door.

I followed closely behind him, past the entrance. He reached over to the side wall and flipped a switch. Lights flickered on up ahead in the church one-by-one, but Walt had only turned a portion of them on so it remained half dark, like dusk falling over our back porches.

At first I thought it wasn't that hot. I suppose if someone

had asked me I would have said it was warm, but nothing like Walt had described. He stepped into the church onto a maroon carpet that stretched down the center aisle and separated the pews. As I followed, I took in my surroundings. When I had come to the barbeque here some years back, they had set up picnic tables down on the beach for the get-together. I never came in here that day, so this was my first time seeing a Catholic church. I don't know what I expected it to look like, but it was much more complicated than my church across town. There was much more for the eye to look at. The stained glass windows were covered with fine artwork, as fine as I'd ever seen. There were paintings and statues everywhere, and a large crucifix hung on the wall up front, demanding attention, probably a little larger than my whole body, with blood covering the body of Jesus on his head, hands and feet. The sight of it took me by surprise. I was used to seeing only the bare cross in my church; this was much more graphic.

As we proceeded up the center aisle, a thought abruptly occurred to me and made my unfamiliar surroundings an afterthought.

It was getting hotter; much hotter.

I felt like I was walking on an asphalt parking lot in the middle of a July day. Walt turned around and glanced at me, probably wondering if I had noticed the rise in temperature.

In the front, left part of the church I could see a section of boxed-in seats. I figured this was where the choir sat. Resting above, I saw the statue. It was about four or five feet tall and ivory white. The woman stood straight up with her arms extending outward, like she was waiting on a hug. Her veil went up over her head and a robe stretched down to her feet.

We didn't have statues like this in my church, but I had seen ones like it before and it didn't look to be out of the ordinary. It looked much like the one I saw in Atlanta when I met with Sister Marie.

When we finally reached the front where the pews ended, I could barely stand it. We'd only entered through the doors two minutes ago and my clothes were literally dripping with sweat. My breaths were heavy and my eyesight had become blurred.

"You okay, Buck?"

"Yeah, sure."

We didn't have to whisper, but we did because it felt unnatural to speak in a normal tone, considering the circumstances. "I know you can feel the difference up here. And look," he said pointing to the back right part of the church, "the wax of those candles is only partially melted, and these up here are completely gone."

I looked back and forth between the two racks of candles. No more than ten yards from where the choir sat, melted wax was caked on the wood floor.

"I see what you're saying," I whispered. "It's hotter than hell in here, and it's sure hotter up here than in the back, but that doesn't mean the statue is what's causing the heat. I still think this is crazy. Let's get out—"

"Touch it, then."

"What?"

"Touch the statue and feel how hot it is."

"It's almost ten feet off the ground."

"Stand on a chair."

Walt didn't wait for me to object as he moved around the

small wall separating the choir from the front aisle. About ten individual chairs were placed in this section. He grabbed one and moved it underneath the statue.

"Well," he said, seeing that I had not moved an inch. My feet stood in quicksand yards from the altar. Now that I was here, I didn't want to touch the statue; I was too afraid Walt would be right.

"Come on over," Walt insisted. "That is, if you can handle it. Do you feel okay? You look terrible."

"I'm fine," I said. "A little bit a' heat isn't going to kill me."

I made my way over to Walt. He braced the chair and gave me a nod.

"Are you not going to touch it too?"

"I touched it on Wednesday. I told you that."

I braced myself and mounted the chair. My feeble bones and off-centered balance forced Walt into helping me up, but when I had stabilized myself, I reached up with my hand and touched the feet of the statue.

A sizzling burn instantly scorched my skin. I ripped my hand off and waved it in the air.

"You can't even keep your hand on it?" Walt asked from below me.

"You told me you'd touched it!" I placed my fingers in my mouth in an attempt to cool them off.

"I did, but I could keep my hand on it for a few seconds before it got too hot."

"I don't think you can do that anymore."

"Ya' see? Then it *is* getting hotter. Let me get up there."

Walt and I switched places. I braced the chair for him as

he climbed up, and within a second he had burned his fingers as well.

"My word in heaven, that's almost twice as hot as it was a few days ago." Walt looked down to me, looking for some kind of response. "What's going on here, Buck?"

I shook my head. "You know I don't know the answer to that. Can we get out of here?"

Walt ignored me and looked back to the statue, as if staring at it would somehow explain the phenomenon. He reached up to touch it again.

"Don't, don't, Walt, don't touch it again. . . ." I couldn't focus. My legs felt light and began to tingle. Bright colors flashed before me. I heard Walt ask if I was all right, but his voice sounded as if it were coming from a distant tunnel.

Not a second later, I blacked out and fell to the ground.

22

PETER SLEPT most of the way as I drove us through southern Georgia and into South Carolina. The day was nearing an end but there was enough light in the sky for me to take in the endless rows of pines off each side of the road. The Southern landscape was unfamiliar to me, but I enjoyed the seclusion and quiet of this part of the country.

Peter eventually offered to drive the last hour or so. I appreciated the offer, as night had fallen, and my eyes were tired from navigating the lonely, back roads we encountered after exiting Interstate 95. We stopped at a small diner in Adams Run, South Carolina, to eat a warm meal and confirm the directions I had mapped out. It turned out we were closer than I thought. The waitress informed us Edisto was only twenty minutes down the winding, two-lane road, and by ten o'clock we were pulling into town. My brother had reserved us a room at a local motel here and in St. Augustine since we weren't sure of our exact itinerary.

Peter put on the turn signal as we approached the first major intersection.

"Go straight, here," I said.

"Don't we take a left to get to the motel?"

"Yes, but we keep straight to make it to the church."

"Why on earth would we go there right now?"

"I don't know, I just—"

"It's too late to do anything tonight, and surely no one will be there to let us in."

"I know. I'm just a little antsy. I want to see it tonight. And if we go there now we'll know where we're going in the morning. I think it's only a few minutes down the road. It won't take long."

Peter took a deep breath and continued straight down the road. We went through the commercialized part of town with shops and stores until we eventually moved down a road twisting between large oak trees draped in Spanish moss.

"Oh," I said as I pointed from the passenger seat. "I think that was it."

Peter slammed on the breaks when he saw me pointing to a wooden sign on the side of the road, reading: "*Our Lady of the Sea, Catholic Church of Edisto Island, South Carolina.*"

He slowly backed up and pulled down a dirt road with bits of rock scattered about on it. For a moment it felt like we were driving into the wilderness, and if it hadn't been for the sign we just saw, I would have thought we'd taken a wrong turn. But soon we had come across a gravel parking lot laid out before a small, stone church, one that looked nearly identical to the church in Jamestown. If I blinked my eyes, I could place this church in Edisto on that grassy hill overlooking the cliff back in Rhode Island and fail to tell the difference, from its size and layout, to the pattern of the stained glass windows interrupting the stone walls, to the red doors at its entrance.

My adrenalin rushed through me like a river. I finally had that gut feeling I was searching for.

Peter pointed across the parking lot. "It's kind of late for that truck to be parked there."

"Someone probably left it here for the night," I replied. "It looks old. Maybe it died."

Peter nodded. "Well, we know where the church is; you want to head to the motel?"

I wanted to get out and walk around, but Peter had compromised by coming here, so I decided to bite my lip. "Sure."

Peter didn't hesitate. He changed gears and thrust the car in reverse so fast that I wondered if he had overlooked the similarities between the two churches. But before he could get us turned around, the church doors flew open. A man backed out of the church, hauling another man out who appeared unconscious, dragging him by his armpits, his feet scraping across the ground. Peter and I looked at each other before bursting out of the car and sprinting across the parking lot.

When we reached them, the lucid one placed the other man on the ground. His shocked eyes met ours. Their aged skin and graying hair told me this elderly man was probably having a heart attack.

"Can you help me get him to the truck?" the conscious one asked

"What happened?" Peter asked.

"I think the heat made him pass out, or . . . Please God! I hope he didn't have a heart attack. Do either of you have any medical expertise?"

"The heat?" I asked.

"Can you just help me get him to the truck?"

Through the open doors of the church, I saw a statue of Mary. I stumbled towards the church, but Peter yelled, "Paul! We have to help him!"

Turning around, I saw Peter standing helplessly over the other two men. I hurried over to the man lying on the ground and touched his forehead. Feeling his roasting skin, I motioned toward the car. "Peter, go grab our thermos of water." I took off my coat and placed it under the elderly man's head. Peter returned with the water, unscrewed the top, and poured a few drops onto the man's head.

"What's his name?" I asked.

"Buck, his name is Buck Washington."

"And you?"

"I'm Walt Henderson."

"How long ago did he pass out, Walt?"

"Not long ago. About two minutes."

I grabbed Buck's wrist and checked his pulse. It was faint, but there. "Buck!" I gently slapped his face. "Can you hear me, Buck?" His eyes opened, but only for an instant. He groaned and licked his cracked lips. I poured a small bit of water into his mouth and over his forehead again. He drank some of it but spit the rest up. "I think this is good," I assured Walt. "At least he's regaining consciousness. Maybe he just fainted. Buck," I yelled, focusing back on the sick man, "can you open your eyes again for me?" He struggled. "How many fingers am I holding up, Buck?"

He squinted. "Three, I think."

"I guess that's good too," Peter said from behind me, confirming Buck had answered correctly.

"What do you think?" Walk asked. "You think I can take him home?"

"Maybe we should take him to the hospital," I suggested.

"I'm fine," Buck mumbled, though I wasn't even sure he knew where he was.

"I think the heat must've drawn up his temperature," Walt said, feeling his friend's forehead. "I don't have time to explain it, but it's almost two hundred degrees in that church right now. I think if we get him home and get a cold towel around his head he'll feel better. He's not going to like me very much if he wakes up in a hospital bed; probably already is mad with me for bringing him here. Can you follow me to his home and help me lift him into bed? We only live a few minutes down the road."

I glanced back at the open church doors, wanting to journey inside. But I knew I had to help. We carried Buck over to Walt's pick-up twenty yards away before realizing that wasn't going to work. Buck clearly needed to lie down, and Walt refused to put him in the bed of his truck, for fear that he could slide around and hit his head.

"We could lie him down in the back of our car," I suggested. "It's got soft, cloth seats. If we're following you over there we might as well put him in our car."

Walt thought this over for a few seconds before agreeing. We carried Buck over to our rental car and gently laid him down in the back seat. Walt looked us over one last time before returning to lock the church doors and climbing into his truck. We pulled away from the church and got back onto the main drag of shops and restaurants in a matter of minutes. It was getting late but I didn't notice. I wanted to help these two men as much as we could, however mostly I wanted to ask about the heat inside the church. I could tell Peter was deep in thought beside me, leaving little conversation between us.

Ten minutes later, we reached an abandoned area. Walt's truck pulled in to a rocky driveway in front of a small cottage, much of it covered in ivy. When we climbed out of the car, I felt the salty air sticking to my skin and heard the ocean waters tumbling on the opposite side of the house.

"Sounds like Buck has some seaside property, here," I said to Walt as he approached our car.

"Yep, we both do."

I looked next door, noticing in the darkness another small home. "You guys are neighbors?"

"Have been for years. This one is Buck's house; let's get him into bed."

Buck could walk a little on his own now, but Peter and I braced him by throwing his arms over our shoulders as we made our way up his gravel sidewalk. He would speak occasionally, however his mind was still cloudy. For a moment it sounded as though he was attempting to apologize in advance for his cluttered home.

The four of us entered his small home, filled quaintly with aged furniture, framed pictures adorning the walls, and a messy kitchen that showed Buck was a single man. In the one and only bedroom, we laid Buck on his mattress as Walt went and got some ice and a wet wash cloth. The three of us sat quietly in the bedroom, making sure he drifted off into a sleep that would help him recuperate. When we felt Buck was okay to leave by himself, we exited the room. Walt offered to get us some water and left for the kitchen.

I whispered to Peter while we were alone. "We need to ask this guy some questions, don't you think?"

Peter didn't reply, and a moment later Walt had returned with our water, inviting us to sit down in Buck's den. When we took our places on the couch, a dusty odor rose up from the green cushions. It wasn't a bad smell, but rather a peculiar one that reminded me of the distinct scent of my grandfather's house.

"I reckon you boys were lookin' for Father Harris tonight?" Walt asked as he sat down across from us.

"If that's your parish priest, then yes, we were," I answered. "But I was hoping we could ask you some questions first, now that we're here."

"All right."

"You said it was almost two hundred degrees in your church."

"That's right."

"Was the heat coming from a strange source?"

Walt's dumbfounded expression and slow nod said more than words.

"A statue?" I asked.

He nodded again, his eyes as wide as clams.

I explained what we had been through in the last few days, or at least as much as I could without overstepping our orders to keep things under wraps. I told him about the church in Rhode Island and the statue there, but didn't reveal anything about Donald. Walt was kind enough to answer all our questions despite being overwhelmed. He laid out the time frame for when the statue in Edisto began to give off heat, and tried to describe what he had seen and felt over the last weeks.

Peter remained silent throughout my explanation as he stared at Walt with vacant eyes.

Before long, Walt had brought up the most important matter surrounding these two statues.

"I don't suppose you boys know *why* the statues are becoming so hot?"

"No," I said. "I was hoping we could find out when we found this second statue."

As I voiced my admission, Peter blinked and seemed to regain a sense of reality. He focused on Walt. The elderly man must have felt the stare. Walt turned and looked at Peter, their eyes locking for a moment. Something came into Peter's face, but disappeared just as soon as it had come.

Walt turned back to me. "Well, no matter what the reason is, this has to be some kind of strange miracle."

I saw Peter shaking his head out of the corner of my eye. Walt had apparently noticed it too. "You don't think so?" he asked.

"Let me ask you something," Peter said leaning forward. "Are the people of your parish frightened by this?"

"Yeah, most were a little scared, especially the women. One lady figured it was a sign of the apocalypse."

"And you said your priest has locked the doors until further notice?"

"He did."

"Then tell me how any part of this is a miracle?"

"Peter," I interjected, "please don't start this right now."

"What do you mean?" Walt asked, ignoring me and focusing on Peter.

"I don't see how this is some miraculous sign when

people are scared half to death, and the doors of churches are being locked. It's a pretty strange god who runs people out of churches, don't you think? What if this starts happening all over the world?"

"I guess you're entitled to your opinion, but that seems a strange thing to hear from a priest."

"Well, your sense of order for the world will be restored shortly when I leave the priesthood."

"You're leaving the priesthood?" Walt asked.

Peter didn't respond.

"Why? If you don't mind me asking."

Peter mashed his lips together and refused to explain. I spoke up. "Peter's had a rough go of it lately. He's not leaving for sure. He's just taking—"

"Don't you dare speak for me, Paul."

"Peter," I pleaded, "I know this situation is scaring and frustrating you; it scares me too. But why are you so adamant in finding the negative aspects of this? I feel like anything could happen at this point and you wouldn't even consider what message God could be trying to send through these statues."

"There's no message here. This is only about confusing and scaring people. God could be using his time in a lot better ways than this."

"You act as if God is the one who's let you down with *his* behavior," Walt interjected, "instead of the other way around."

Peter scowled. "You don't know me, sir. You have no idea what I've been through."

I tried to move the conversation back to the statues and away from Peter.

"I'm sorry, Walt. Peter obviously has some things going

on that don't involve you. He doesn't mean these things, but maybe for now we should—"

"Why don't you come outside with me," Walt said, staring straight at Peter and interrupting me.

"Why?" Peter asked.

"Please come out on the porch." Walt stood up and held out his hand toward the door.

I watched, baffled, as the two men stepped outside and left me alone. I was tempted to eavesdrop, but thought it better not to. Walt must have had some reason for wanting to speak with Peter in private, and I wanted to respect that.

23

I WASN'T sure how long it took me to regain my wits after passing out, but I vaguely remembered trying to lift my eyelids and not being able to. I heard unfamiliar voices and figured I might have been in an ambulance. But when I finally did pry my eyes open, I discovered I was in someone's car, a sedan, lying down in the back with my legs scrunched up against the side door. My blurred vision was making me nauseous, so I drifted off again into a sea of darkness.

I eventually awoke to the rickety squeak of my bed frame and the cotton feel of my blanket. As I sat up off the mattress, a damp wash cloth fell from my forehead to the covers. I rubbed my eyes and gazed around my room, then peered out the window to see it was still dark out.

I heard movement coming from outside my bedroom. "Walt?" My voice sounded like it was rolling off a brillo pad as it left my throat. "That you?"

Footsteps approached the doorway. A figure moved forward.

"Hello. It's Mr. Washington, right?"

I blinked several times, trying to determine who this

man was. He stood before me in a black outfit from head to toe, except for the white collar around his neck. His face was youthful, probably about thirty-five if I took aim at guessing, and his short hair was combed perfectly to the side.

"Am I about to die?"

The man laughed and pulled up a seat by my bedside. "No, I think you'll live. Please, lay back down. Do you feel okay?"

I followed his advice, returning my head slowly to the pillows. He picked up the wash cloth and placed it on my forehead.

"I suppose I'm okay," I finally answered him. "Other than the fact it feels like someone took a sledge hammer to my head. Now, who are you? And where's Walt? And how'd I get back here in my bed?"

"Let's do one at a time, Mr. Washington."

"Buck," I corrected him.

"Okay, Buck. I'm Father Paul, but you can just call me Paul if you like. We were in the parking lot when Walt dragged you out of the church. You were in such bad condition that we had to help get you home. Walt is actually outside right now, speaking with my friend, Father Peter."

I eyed him suspiciously, wondering if everything he had said was the truth. But he was a priest; how could I not trust him?

"Was that your car I was in?"

"It was," he answered. "Or, it's my rental. We're from out of town. We considered taking you to the hospital, but you were answering our questions correctly and you seemed to be all right."

"You said I answered your questions?"

"Yes, like, 'how many fingers am I holding up?' Things like that."

I laughed. "Boy, I don't recall that one bit. So you're from out of town?"

"Yes, we're from up north, just outside of Boston. We just got into Edisto tonight."

"Well, I may not know much about the travels and schedules of priests, but what were you guys doing outside that church so late? Walt told me no one would be there."

Paul leaned back in his chair. "That's kind of a long story. But let's just say I know why you passed out."

I thought back to when I stood inside the church. "You know about the statue?"

He nodded.

"How? I thought you said you just got into town tonight? I thought Walt said his parish hadn't told anyone about the statue yet?" I didn't give Father Paul a chance to answer before I realized I was curious about something else. "What's he talking about with your friend?"

"Buck, I know you may not believe this, but I have no idea what they're talking about out there. In a way, I'm as confused as you are about this whole thing."

The slam of my screen door stopped him from going any further.

"That must be Walt and Peter." Paul stood up and left the room. I heard the low rumble of them speaking in my den, but couldn't make out what they were discussing. A few minutes later they all returned to my bedroom.

I was relieved when I saw Walt.

"Hey there, buddy," he said as he knelt down by my bed and grabbed my hand. "How you feelin'?"

"I'm okay."

"I'm sorry I made you go inside the church. I shouldn't have done that. It was dangerous. I don't know what I would've done if something more serious had happened."

"It's okay, Walt. I'm fine, really, I am. You had no way of knowing my feeble, old body would keel over like that."

He laughed but I could tell he felt guilty. "I assume you met Paul, here, and this is Peter."

The man named Peter came over and shook my hand. "It's nice to meet you," he said, his voice lacking any effort. "I'm glad you're feeling better."

"Yeah, thanks." I gripped his hand and stared into his eyes. They seemed familiar. "Have we met before?"

"I don't think so. I don't see how we ever could have."

"I suppose you're right. But where'd you grow up, out of curiosity? Maybe I know someone in your family. You got the look of someone I might've known."

"I don't see how that's relevant, Mr. Washington. Paul," he said, turning his focus to the other side of the room, "I think it's time we get to our motel."

"Sorry if I offended you," I said, surprised by his sudden curtness, "but can someone tell me what's going on before y'all leave. I'd like to hear about the part of the evening I missed."

Paul approached the bed and extended his hand. "I'd like to, but Peter's right, it's late and we have to get up early in the morning. Maybe Walt can fill you in on everything."

I shook his hand and said goodbye to the two priests. They walked out of my bedroom and left me to my rest. I heard

Walt thank them for helping take care of me, and I heard them
thank Walt for the information he had provided. A few minutes later their car had pulled out of the driveway. Walt came
back to my doorway, his body covered in shadows cast by the
light from my den. "It's been one helluva' night, hasn't it, pal?"

"Any chance you filling me in on the half I missed?"

"Sure, that is, if you don't think you need to get your rest."

"I'm fine, but it'd be nice if I could get some food in me."

"I think I can handle that."

Walt helped me into the den where I sat down at my
table. He made us both a fried bologna sandwich and got me
a Coke to awaken my senses. We exchanged small talk about
how I was feeling and what we thought had happened to me. I
made it clear I was okay and that I was through talking about
it. Walt should have known better than anyone that old men
don't enjoy discussing their health. We always felt fine, so no
reason to ask.

"All right," I said as I bit down into my sandwich, "what
in the world happened tonight? I'm a little curious about what
those priests were doin' outside your church at such a late hour,
especially since you said no one would be there."

"It'll be hard for you to believe me after what I just heard."

"After what I saw tonight, I'll believe anything."

Walt took a sip of water to wash down his food and wiped
his mouth with a napkin. "Well," he began, "when you fainted,
I thought you'd up and died on me. I didn't know what to do
at first, but then I realized I needed to get you out of that heat,
so I dragged you out of the church as fast I could. When I got
us outside, I just about fell over at the sight of those two men
standing there."

"Did you figure out what they were doing in the parking lot?"

"I'm getting there."

I took another bite of my sandwich so I wouldn't inter-rupt him.

"Since I was more concerned about you at the time, I didn't ask what they were doing there. But I was sure glad to see them. They checked your pulse and got you some water, and it seemed you'd only fainted. We talked about taking you to the hospital but I felt you'd be all right, so I got them to help carry you and asked that they follow me back here to get you into bed. I agreed to put you in their car so you could lie down in their soft, back seat, rather than the bed of my truck."

"I was wondering how I ended up in their car."

"Well, they seemed trustworthy, and they'd been real helpful up until that point. Anyway, they followed me back over here and we put you in bed. We gave you some medicine for your fever and laid a cold wash cloth on your head. Then we went into your den so you could sleep, and Buck, I couldn't even fathom what they told me they were doing in Edisto." I had a mouth full of food, but forgot to keep chewing it as I waited for Walt to finish. "It turns out these two priests were coming down to South Carolina on a very specific mission. They were in search of a heated statue, Buck, a heated statue of Mary."

"A heated statue? You can't be serious."

"I know. I still can't believe it. But it gets even stranger. They were in Rhode Island this past week investigating another statue of Mary that had begun giving off heat, just like the one in my church. I knew it was the statue causing the heat. Didn't I tell you?"

"Did they know why the statues were doing this?"

"Don't think so. They seem just as baffled as us."

"What else did they tell you?"

"They couldn't reveal much because they were under orders from their superiors, but they said the statue in Rhode Island started heating up a couple weeks back, about the same time as the statue here. As we compared stories, it sounded like the statue up there was a little hotter than our statue here, but I suppose it'll take more time studying them to figure that out. Either way we both guessed it was over two-hundred degrees inside the churches."

I set down my sandwich, staring blankly ahead. "It's a wonder something like this would happen in Edisto. It's such a simple, small town. And no offense, but that church of yours is tiny. Wouldn't you think this would happen at some grand cathedral?"

Walt responded after a short pause. "Jesus was born in a stable, Buck, not a palace."

I nodded and moved on. "I don't see how they knew to leave Rhode Island and come here."

"They didn't say, probably weren't allowed to tell me. But the church up there was apparently called Our Lady of the Sea, just like my church. I guess that's your connection. But also, they told me Edisto wasn't the first place they'd visited. I reckon they'd been to a few other places before coming here."

I stood up and took my plate to the sink. After I had washed and dried it, I returned to the table and rubbed my face. "I feel like this is some sign, like something's about to happen. God, I hope this ain't the rapture. I suppose the news will want to cover this. You think they'll be coming to report on it soon?"

"Can't say for sure. Father Paul and Father Peter said the parish in Rhode Island was keeping quiet about what was going on, and we're doing the same here, at least for now. People will find out about it eventually, though. Stuff like this doesn't stay secret for long."

"So what happens now?"

"I'm meeting with Paul and Peter in the morning, over at the church. But I'm supposed to go get my local priest and they're going to fill him in on everything. I guess we'll try and go back in the church again. If it's still as hot as it was tonight, I think more people will be coming here to investigate."

Walt and I decided we needed a few drinks to settle our nerves. I grabbed my cooler and filled it up with beer and ice while he walked over to his place and got Sam. I put on an easy listening, brass instrument record from the forties that we'd grown accustomed to listening to, turning my speakers up just loud enough so the music could reach our ears on my back porch. Dawn wasn't far off in the horizon, but for now we could still enjoy the glittering constellations above as an autumn wind chilled us through our Corduroy coats. This situation normally lent itself to a game of checkers, but our minds were too busy for that. We spoke more about the statues and the visiting priests, and tossed around a few theories we had. But we both knew we were only taking stabs in the dark.

When I thought we'd all but exhausted the topic, I recalled something else about the evening that I had intended to ask Walt about.

"Say Walt, why'd you go outside and speak with one of those priests while the other one stayed inside with me?"

Walt thought for a moment before answering. "I forgot about that with everything else going on."

"Well?"

Walt took a swig of his beer. "As the three of us sat in your den, I began to notice something about one of those priests, the one named Peter."

"Sure, I remember which one he was. He seemed a little downtrodden compared to the other one. And he snapped at me when I asked where he grew up."

"Yeah, I noticed."

"So did you figure out what was wrong?"

"In some ways, yes. I didn't talk to him but ten minutes, though; you can't learn all there is to know about someone in that short a time. But he told me he was leaving the priesthood."

"Really? I always figured if someone became a priest, he did it for life."

"Most do, but I guess some go on to do other things. And I told him if he felt God was calling him to do something else with his life, then so be it, but I still lectured him a good bit."

"You lectured him? About what?"

"That boy had a lot of scorn for God."

"Scorn for God, ya' say? From a *priest?*"

"I know it sounds strange, but as they sat telling me about the statue in Rhode Island and their investigation, Paul figured that statue heating up was some kind of miracle. That's the way I feel, too, I think. But Peter seemed angered by it all, or maybe he was just angry in general, I don't know. He questioned why God would do such a thing, keeping parishioners

out of their church and scaring people like this. Course I have
to admit, I don't have an answer for why this is happening, but
I wouldn't let him sit there and say the things he was saying,
so I took him outside and spoke with him. I don't really know
what came over me. I just felt the need to set him straight."

"What'd you say?"

"To tell you the truth, I doubt I helped him a bit. It's just,
he said he'd been through a lot in his life, and seen a lot of
pain. He said he was through trying to make peace with God
for all that had happened to him. Anytime I tried to ask about
his past he told me to leave it alone, 'cause there was no way
I could understand what he'd been through. He was probably
right. After all, he's only a bit more than a stranger to me. But
I told him that wasn't important, because no matter what life
throws at him, or me, or you, or anyone else, all we can do is
just keep carrying our cross."

"What do you mean?"

I leaned up in my rocking chair.

"We all got a cross to bear, Buck, a cross of suffering, confusion, addiction, anger, jealousy, loneliness, illness, and all
the like. Maybe I've done more thinking on this than most
because of Olivia and my boy, but the way I see it, some people
lay that cross upon their shoulders by their own doing, like
I did, with the decisions I made that led to my guilt. Others
probably don't deserve the cross they received, like those born
real poor or sick, but it doesn't matter which one of these people we are, because what else can we do except keep movin' up
that hill? We all got our own Calvary to climb; and you know
what the kicker is?"

"What's that?"

"We aren't carrying that cross by ourselves. You know he's right there alongside us. This was all stuff I didn't realize until recently, and I have you to thank for that, Buck. In a strange way your friendship helped me understand all this, understand our life struggles are something we just have to deal with no matter the cost. I figured I'd share that secret with Peter before he gets to be my age and realizes he's wasted his whole life thinking he's lugging that cross by himself. You'd think he'd know that as a priest, but I guess everybody needs reminding."

I appreciated Walt's gratitude but was too embarrassed to acknowledge it.

"Peter said he got what I was trying to say, but that he still didn't understand why God gave some people a cross when they didn't deserve it. The way he was talkin' made me think of that little girl in Costa Rica I help, ya' know, the one I have a picture of over at my place?"

"Oh yeah, I remember her."

"Lord knows she doesn't deserve to suffer like she does, and when I told Peter about her, he said that's exactly the kind of grief he was talking about, the kind that weighs on him so heavy. He asked how she could be given that life."

"What'd you tell him?"

"I told him don't nobody *truly* know the answer to that question, but you know who else didn't deserve the cross he was given?"

We both knew.

"It's not whether or not we deserve our cross. It's how we carry it. I tried my hardest to help Peter see that."

I looked out over the sea. Everything was dark except for the salty foam of each tumbling wave. "I think I know what you mean," I said looking back to him, "about us all having a cross to bear. I suppose if Jesus can come down here and carry his, we shouldn't expect not to have one, too."

"That's the way I see it. I told him it was his life to live, but the worst thing he could do is shut himself off from God altogether. When they left, he didn't seem to be thinking any differently, so I don't think I did a bit a' good." Walt shrugged and took a swig of beer. "Truth is, we all struggle, the only difference is what we struggle with. But if you turn away from God you got no chance. I fight depression and regret everyday, but there wouldn't even be a fight to speak of if I didn't keep God on my side; I'd just be overrun by my demons. I wanted to help that boy, and let him know he's not fighting his struggles alone. You think I gave him some good advice, Buck?"

"I sure do, Walt. All that stuff you said was real profound. I didn't know you had it in you."

"I didn't either. It felt like it wasn't even me talking to him."

I didn't know what else to say about the matter, so I held out my bottle of beer, prompting him to tap it with his own bottle.

"Cheers," we said in unison.

We both polished off the last of our lagers before Walt got up to walk back to his place for the evening. As usual, Sam followed him without being told to. As I rose from my rocker and reached for the screen door, I heard Walt from twenty yards away.

"Hey, Buck?"

"Yeah?"

"Just a couple weeks ago would've been my boy's birthday."

I stared into the darkness where his voice was coming from. "What do you make of that?"

I thought for a second before responding. "Not sure what you're gettin' at, neighbor."

Silence came from the darkness, until he said, "Yeah, I don't know either." I then heard his feet shuffle away towards his home, over the grass and sand.

24

WHEN MY alarm clock went off at seven o'clock the next morning, I felt like my body had sunk inside the mattress. There was a brief period when I couldn't remember where I was or what I was supposed to be doing. But when I smelled the distinct odor and felt the glossy touch of the hotel covers, it all came back to me. I remembered we had made plans to meet Walt at the church this morning, along with his local priest.

Peter slept in a bit longer, while I went out and got us breakfast. As I tooled around Edisto searching for food and my morning newspaper, I wondered what Peter could be thinking now that we had found the second statue. It seemed like his feelings toward Donald's claims and this phenomenon should've changed, considering what we now knew. But when we hopped in the car at eight-fifteen to head across town, I had something else on my mind that took precedence over the statues. I couldn't help wondering what Walt and Peter had spoken about on Buck's back porch. Peter didn't seem to be acting any differently since returning from their talk, and he didn't reveal what the talk had been about. Every bone in my

body wanted to ask him about it, but I decided I should concentrate on one thing at a time, for we were only minutes away
from pulling into the parking lot of Our Lady of the Sea.

"There's something I want to say before we get there,"
Peter suddenly said.

"All right."

"Pull over for a second."

I navigated the car to the side of the dirt road, just before
the wooden sign directing people towards the church. We both
sat still for a moment as the dust particles floating around our
car became illuminated by rays of sunlight.

"I've been pretty hardheaded with this whole thing over
the last few days. I realize that now, and I'm sorry."

When Peter didn't continue I felt the need to respond.
"It's a hard thing to make sense of."

He looked out the window, toward the coastal, Carolina
brush. "If we go in that church and there really is a statue of
Mary giving off heat, I don't see how I can deny anymore that
this is something beyond us, beyond our world. It may not cure
my doubt and bitterness, but I know sometimes things happen for a reason. I have to admit that, whether I like it or
not. Maybe there is a purpose behind these heated statues, and
maybe it's a purpose that's meant to do good. I suppose that
will all play itself out, and hopefully one day we'll know for
sure, maybe even today"

I nodded and shifted the car into drive, wondering in the
back of my mind if I owed Walt a great debt of gratitude.

As we came around a bend in the oak trees, we saw the
church for the first time in the light of day. Out front we saw
Walt standing by his pick-up truck, along with a young priest

with sandy, blond hair. We parked near them and unhooked our seatbelts. "You ready for this?" I asked Peter.

"I think I have to be, don't I?"

We introduced ourselves to Father Harris, a younger priest with a soft face and deep, brown eyes. It wasn't often that Peter and I were in the position of being the "veteran" priest, but it was evident from the onset that Father Harris was shaken by what was unfolding at his parish. I assumed Edisto was normally a quiet place, a town where excitement was as absent to the residents here as their palmetto trees were to us in Massachusetts. These last few weeks seemed to have taken their toll on the young, jittery priest.

"Have you contacted anyone about the statue?" I asked him.

"Not yet. I had planned to call the Bishop in Charleston today, but . . . but when Walt showed up this morning and told me about all this, about you two and the other statue, I decided to wait and see what happens today."

"Why don't we head inside," I said. "We need to see this statue for ourselves if we are going to report this back to our superiors."

"Sure," Father Harris replied as he reached into his pocket for the key. "I understand."

"Only if it's safe enough," Walt interjected. "Don't forget what happened to Buck last night. They went into the church in Rhode Island with the fire department, Father Harris. Remember how I told you that?"

Father Harris glared at Walt. We knew Walt had confessed to everything from last night. The tension between them made it awkward for everyone, but I could understand why Father Harris didn't want people breaking into his church at all hours of the night, especially with what was going on.

"Well," he said, "if I recall their story correctly, they had a parishioner in the local fire department. We don't have that luxury here. For now, I'd like to keep the rest of the town away. Calling the authorities would ruin that. Do you mind us going in by ourselves?"

"Not at all," I answered. "I'd prefer that, actually. We won't stay long if it's as hot as you and Walt say it is."

Father Harris nodded and turned the key over, shifting the deadbolt and unlocking the doors. He walked in first, slowly and cautiously, with me behind him and Walt and Peter in the rear. As we entered the dark narthex, apprehension crept over me. I wanted so badly for the statue to be as hot as Walt had described, to help confirm the phenomenon and strengthen Peter's feelings about believing in this. But if the statue *was* hot, there was still the matter of why this was happening and what event would "come to pass" before this would all be over. On the surface I was captivated by what I had witnessed, even inspired. But like so many of the parishioners at Our Lady of the Sea in Jamestown and here in Edisto, I was frightened. What if some of the things people had feared were becoming a reality? What if this really was a sign of the apocalypse? What if God *was* angry with us and the Virgin Mary was trying to warn us? What if Peter was right and this phenomenon was going to start happening all over the world? What if thousands of people were going to be kept out of their church? Why would God want that?

Despite my fear, I moved forward without hesitation. We hadn't taken five steps when I realized the similarities between the two churches didn't just apply to the outside of the structures. Much of the inside of this church looked like a replica of the one in Jamestown, including the artwork, stained-glass windows, light fixtures, and general layout of the pews. The only difference I noticed was the area where the statue of Mary stood. While the one in Rhode Island was tucked away in an enclave right above our line of sight, this one rested on a podium jutting out from the wall some ten feet off the ground.

As we moved up the center aisle, I waited for my body to be suffocated by a blanket of heat. But there was nothing. I turned around and glanced at Peter and Walt; their expressions also showed they felt nothing out of the ordinary. "Should we have felt something by now?" I asked Father Harris.

He stopped walking and put his hands on his hips, prompting the rest of us to halt midway up the church's center aisle. His eyes stared up at the statue, now twenty feet away. "We could barely walk ten steps up this aisle yesterday."

We walked forward some more as my heart sank deep into a gloomy part of my chest. With each step and breath I took, I prayed that a wave of heat would engulf us all. But within another minute, we were standing directly under the statue and still all was normal. Father Harris mounted a chair from the choir and felt the feet of Mary.

"It's completely fine, feels about like room temperature." He looked down at me, his eyes stretched wide. "I don't know whether to be relieved or disappointed."

He climbed down and began to speak with Walt about the sudden change, while I did my best to avoid eye contact with Peter. After several minutes of discussion with Walt and

Father Harris, I couldn't fight the temptation any longer. I looked toward Peter. I didn't see what I expected, his anger or his frustration, but rather a great sadness within him. It was as if he truly wanted the statue to be as hot as Walt had described, no matter how much confusion it would've caused. Peter turned and slowly walked out of the church without saying anything. Walt's eyes followed Peter all the way to the doors. After a few more minutes of studying the various parts of the church, the three of walked back outside as well.

Peter sat in the passenger seat of the car with his head turned out toward the woods, away from the church. He gave no sign he would get back out to say goodbye to Father Harris and Walt. I tried to do it on his behalf.

"Thanks for meeting us here," I began. "I'm at a loss for words at this point."

"You believe us, don't you?" Walt asked. "You know that statue was as hot as fire, right?" Father Harris's expression bore the same questions.

"Yes," I finally responded. "I believe you. There's no way you would have been able to fabricate this on a whim, and we knew, or, I knew there was a second statue out there somewhere. I can't tell you how I knew that quite yet, but I'm sure I'll be able to eventually. I'll contact the church in Rhode Island and see what's going on there. Who knows what I'll find?"

"Do you think it will have cooled off too?" Walt asked.

"I won't be surprised if it has."

Father Harris frowned. "Why do you think they all of a sudden returned to normal?" The three of us stood still, our thoughts tangled with the sounds of the distant waves.

"Maybe the purpose of the heated statues has been fulfilled," Walt said. "Whatever it was."

I smiled. "Maybe so."

I exchanged information with Father Harris and assured him I would be in touch after I had spoken with Father Powell in Rhode Island and Father Chase back in Worcester. Father Harris walked back to Walt's truck in a daze, no doubt trying to figure out what had exactly happened at his parish over the last few weeks.

I stood alone with Walt now. "Thanks for all your help, Walt. I don't know what will come of it all, but I appreciate your cooperation and input."

"No, no, thank you. You and Peter helped me take care of Buck. I would've struggled to do that without you two." We shook hands. "You think he'll be okay?" Walt asked, motioning his head toward Peter.

I turned and glanced at my friend. "I don't know. I hope so."

"Well, I know he doesn't care to say goodbye to me, but will you tell him I'll be praying for him, as soon as I get to my morning prayers."

"I sure will, Walt. It was nice to meet you."

I walked away, wondering what I would say to Peter when I entered the car. I sat down in the driver's seat and shut the door. Peter turned towards me.

"I'm no shepherd, Paul. Please get me out of here."

Peter and I flew to Boston later that day. After taking the commuter rail back to campus in Worcester, I called Father Powell in Jamestown. By no surprise to anyone, the statue there had also returned to normal. Father Powell informed us that Donald had not revealed any new messages, and frankly, Father Powell was happy for that. All he wanted was for things to return to the way they were. I couldn't blame him. We told him to contact us if anything changed, but I knew we wouldn't hear from him again.

Over the next weeks, news of the heated statues was leaked to the local media in Rhode Island and in South Carolina. Several stories were done on the news and in the papers, but without any hard evidence the stories died without much interest. As expected, they spun it to look as if both parishes had gone mad.

It seemed from the moment we landed in Boston Peter was through discussing the statues, leaving in the past like so many other things that had saddened him throughout the years. He didn't accompany me to meet with Father Chase the next day, nor did he speak about it with anyone else when news spread of the happening.

Peter spent the next week working out tentative plans for his future. Like they had agreed upon before our trip down south, he and Father Chase worked out a sabbatical that would last six months. At the end of that period, if Peter hadn't changed his feelings about his faith and his calling, he would have to leave for good.

Father Chase was kind enough to call a good friend on Peter's behalf to help him during his hiatus from his calling. Peter would live above a garage in Floral Park, New York, just outside the city, and work on the docks with Father Chase's friend every other day. Each week he would also be required to participate in various seminars and workshops set up for priests on sabbatical. Father Chase thought this was the best thing for Peter. Experiencing a "normal" job for a brief period would hopefully clear his mind, but at the same time Father Chase made sure Peter would have constant contact with the Church. The various classes Peter would be involved in were set up to let him discuss his issues with psychiatric counselors, as well as other priests. His vows would still be followed, but for six months he could get away and hopefully cleanse his weathered soul. Father Chase was confident this plan would benefit Peter greatly, and he would be back before the six months were even up.

I, on the other hand, wasn't so sure. Father Chase had not been with Peter over the last several weeks. He had not seen firsthand the bitterness and confusion welling up inside Peter. The things he had said, the miracles he had denied, the unfamiliar feel of his company; it was too much for me to believe Peter would return.

And so I stood outside our house on campus, waiting for Peter to pack up his things so he could make his way to New York. I hadn't slept much since the day we returned from Edisto. All I could think about was what I would say to Peter when he left. That moment was upon me before I had figured out how to say goodbye.

He exited the house, duffle bag in hand, and met me at the end of our sidewalk.

"Want to take a walk?" he asked me.

"Sure."

We turned toward campus on the jagged and broken sidewalk we knew so well.

"Are you sure you got everything?" I asked.

"I think so. You don't own too much when you've been a priest for over a decade."

It was strange to see him in normal clothes. His blue jeans, cotton T-shirt and tan jacket would look normal on anyone else, but not on Peter. I was reminded of the last time I saw him dressed this way, the night I caught him leaving for the bus station. So much had happened since then, but yet here we were again. What good had come from all this? Maybe Peter would've been better served had I let him leave that night. I felt my efforts over the last weeks had only pushed him even further away.

"I want to say I'll keep in touch during this break I'm taking, but I don't want to promise something when I don't know if I can keep my word. I've decided," he took a deep breath, "I've decided if I'm truly going to get away from this life for a little while, it won't help if I'm constantly calling and visiting."

"I understand. Will you stay in New York the whole time?"

"I'm not sure. I've looked over the different things Father Chase has given me the chance to do. Some of the workshops and seminars involve traveling. Those decisions will hopefully work themselves out."

"Well, I think this will help. I'm happy for you."

"No you're not."

I smiled. "How do you always know when I'm lying?"

"You look awkward when you're not telling the truth."

"I'll have to work on that."

"No, please don't."

After a few minutes we curved around the classroom buildings and approached the church.

"Do you think you'll come back?" I asked.

"I don't want to answer that right now. Give it time."

I nodded, looking to the ground as the wind blew fallen leaves atop my shoes. "You want to hear something strange?" Peter asked.

"Sure."

"You'd think I would have constantly thought about those statues over the last few days, but I haven't at all. You know what's occupied my mind when I think back on our two trips?"

"What's that?"

"It's something Walt said on that back porch. He suddenly began to talk about a little girl in Costa Rica he helps out through a program with his church. He sends her letters and money, and even exchanges pictures with her."

I thought back to the little girl Peter had mentioned weeks earlier. I had dreamt about her the night before we left for Rhode Island, and thought about her several other times in the following days. I remember thinking that I wished Peter had never met her.

"Why did he bring her up?" I asked.

"I guess I mentioned that I'd been through a lot of stuff that was out of my control. I think he brought her up because he was trying to comfort me, trying to show me that everyone suffers, even those who don't deserve it."

"Had he ever visited her?"

"He said when he started the program about a year ago, he had always been afraid of traveling places. Just a strange phobia, I guess. But about two months ago he seriously considered going down there to finally meet her."

"And did he go?"

Peter shook his head.

"Why not?"

He looked around, hesitating. "The day Walt was going to buy a plane ticket he went to the doctor because of some pain he'd been having in his stomach. He got diagnosed with cancer, Paul."

I gasped. "That's terrible."

"He's starting chemotherapy next week. He hadn't even told that friend of his. Buck was his name, I think, wasn't it?"

I nodded.

"I really can't imagine why I was the first person he chose to tell." Peter paused briefly, letting our thoughts fill the silence. "He went on a little more about the girl he helps out, but I just sat there with a scowl on my face. I didn't even tell him about the girl I had met in Costa Rica, and how seeing her situation was what brought back all my bitterness. I've been thinking about her constantly over these last few weeks, but I suppose I resented him for trying to lecture me; that's why I didn't say anything."

We moved through the garden gate on the side of the church. Peter walked before me on the narrow path between the flowers, but altered our normal walk when he turned right on the path and approached a bench stationed on the east side of the garden. He sat down and I did the same.

"When we got back to the motel that night," Peter went on, "I thought about everything that happened in Rhode Island and Edisto and decided Walt mentioning that little girl was too much. After that, I had to admit something strange was happening, like I did that day in the car, on our way back to the church in Edisto. But when we went back in that church and the statue wasn't giving off heat anymore, it felt like a slap in the face. Do you know what I mean?"

I did, but I didn't want to admit it. In some ways, my faith had been challenged by this whole episode as well.

"So you didn't say *anything* to Walt about that girl you met in Costa Rica? Even after he talked about the girl he knew?"

"Nope, not a word. But it's strange, isn't it? Of all the things he could have said right then, and all the countries he could have sponsored a child in. What do you make of that?"

"I have no idea. Maybe . . ." I paused. "Maybe you should think about that while you're gone."

He stood up from the bench and threw his duffle bag over his shoulder. I stood up with him.

"I'm sorry I wasn't able to do more to help you, Peter. I know I can't change your past, but I wish I could've helped you make sense of why it all happened."

He shook his head. "No, Paul. Please don't say that. None of this was your fault. No one could've helped me make sense of my life. All the pain started with something I'll never know the answer to." He stopped and looked toward the sky, squinting in the sunlight. "I'll never know why my family didn't want me after I was born. I've never felt like I belonged anywhere, never felt like I found a home. That was the starting point of all the confusion in my life. I feel like they must've thought I'd have a better life somewhere else, but I wish they wouldn't have thought that."

"Well, I wish I could agree, but then I might not have met you."

He smiled and held out his hand. "I want to thank you for

your friendship, Paul, over the last five years, but mainly over the course of these last few days. You've shown what kind of man you are."

I shook his hand and nodded, but couldn't offer anything in return. My emotions wouldn't let me.

He walked away down the rock path of the garden, but before he had taken five strides, he turned back.

"Paul?" He looked me directly in the eyes. "Pray for me."

"Of course, Peter."

He moved down the path and out of sight. I glanced to my right and saw a statue of Mary resting on a concrete base in the garden. Without taking my eyes off her, I walked over and knelt before the statue.

25

SIX MONTHS after that strange night, I stood on the beach late in the afternoon, facing the waters and the boundless sky. My favorite pair of overalls hung on my bare shoulders as the sand blew at my feet in the coastal gusts. In my right hand I held Walt's violin, and in the other, I held a faded photograph. It was my favorite picture, a snapshot taken the day Walt and I went out fishing on my friend's boat, the day Walt almost caught a shark, and the day he told me how Olivia had died and how he had abandoned his son.

I looked out over the drifting tides as I had done so many times before. But the sea was different today. It was calm, with no waves gliding across the surface. The water seemed like thick jelly that had no notion of acting like itself. I suppose I always knew the ocean would be somber in the last days of Walter Henderson's life.

I could put this off no longer, knowing I had made a promise to my friend and it was time to follow through. I moved forward into the first of the waves, the kind that trickle over your feet in a soft and pleasant way. The water was chilled by the winter air that had just begun to fade into spring, but I ignored the cold. I kept my focus straight ahead, not stopping until I was waist deep in the sea.

"Well," I began, "I suppose I've had him for as long as I'm entitled to, and it's time for him to be back with you. He asked me to give you his violin, so that you'd have it when he got up there. I suppose I'm doing the right thing by coming out into these waters." I paused in speaking to Walt's wife as I looked up at the clouds. "I think the seagulls and pelicans will miss Walt's music in the morning, just as much as me, maybe. I thought about learning how to play, but I don't have a musical bone in my body, Olivia, so I wouldn't be doin' anyone any favors." I laughed, but only to help contain my emotions. "My mama always said you don't get appreciated until ya' die, and I think that's true. I'm sure I won't realize all the things Walt's done for me until he's gone, and I'm sorry for that. But assure him that I got everything in order. I went to the bank and saw his lawyer. All his assets are being put together and a check will be sent to that children's home in Aiken, like he wanted. It wasn't much, God bless him, but I'm sure they'll appreciate it. And of course I'll take care of his most prized asset." I turned around and glanced at the back porch. Although he was only a yellow dot from so far away, I saw Walt's sidekick lying down on the steps. I knew in the back of my mind that he was also in the winter of his life, but I couldn't bear to think about that. "I'll take care of Sam. I'll take him on walks, give him his favorite foods and let him sleep in the bed with me. He's been noticeably sad, but he'll be okay. He's strong, like Walt."

I looked down at the picture of Walt and me fishing. It's strange, but I always felt different when I gazed at a picture of someone who had passed on, like they were staring back at me somehow. Although the doctors had said Walt still had a day or two left, he was already gone. The cancer had consumed him so much at this point he hadn't spoken a word in nearly a week.

I folded up the picture and stuffed it down through the hole in Walt's violin. "Anyway," I continued, "I'm sorry I never met you in person, Olivia, but I know we'll have that chance if I ever make it over to the other side. I'm sad Walt's leaving me, but I'm glad you two will get the chance to be together again. He'll be there pretty soon, and I know he'll play this for you as soon as he arrives."

I laid the violin down on the surface of the water and gave it a nudge. It floated delicately out to sea, letting me watch it as I recalled the many mornings I had listened to Walt's music.

Suddenly, in a moment that defied the laws of the earth, a slight wave moved away from the land. It came from behind me, rippling up like a speed bump and taking the violin away. Eventually, the wave fell back into the sea, joining the rest of its brothers. It left the violin on the surface, now fifty yards separated from me.

A few minutes later, I arrived back on the beach. I looked down at my wet overalls suffocating my skin and chilling my bones. I laughed at myself, thinking how big a fool I must have looked like. When I approached Walt's back porch, Sam began to wag his tail, just as he always did, but slower than normal. I sat down and rubbed his head.

Just then, I heard the slam of a car door. I walked to the side of the house along with Sam and saw a man with a ragged beard running up into his disheveled hair. He stood in Walt's driveway in jeans and a flannel shirt, looking around like he was lost. "May I help you?" I yelled to him.

He leaned around the corner of the house and awkwardly waved to me. His steps toward me were slow, as if he were unsure of how to answer my question. I could tell he wondered what I was doing in soaking wet clothes, but he didn't ask about my attire. "Buck Washington, right?"

"That's right. Do I know you?"

"I met you months ago, but you may not remember me."

"I'm sorry, I don't think I do."

"That's okay. Is Walt home? Walter Henderson was his full name. I'd like to speak with him if I could."

"I'm sorry to have to tell you this, but Walt's been in the hospital for over a month now. The doctors say he ain't got but a day or so left."

I tried to recall the few people who had visited Walt over the years, wondering if this was an old friend of his. But despite the familiarity of his eyes, I felt I had never seen this man.

"Oh," he finally said. "I'm sorry. I knew he had cancer, but I didn't know it had progressed so quickly."

I nodded. "Now, how did we meet? And how'd you know Walt?"

"Do you think we can go and sit somewhere for a minute?"

I looked him up and down. "Sure."

I led him over to Walt's back porch where we found a seat on the rocking chairs. He took in his surroundings like his life depended on doing so. "I bet you two played checkers all the time," he finally said.

I looked behind us at the checkerboard leaning up against Walt's rusty lantern. "We did. Got a row of tally marks etched in the porch over yonder that kept track of our record against each other. There's probably a thousand marks carved by my pocket knife in that beat-up, old wood." I fell silent as a sad thought suddenly hit me. "I guess I won't be playin' much anymore."

"I used to love to play that game as a child," he said. "I grew up around a bunch of other children, so I always had someone to play with. I guess I was lucky for that."

I decided I was through with small talk. "Do you mind telling me who you are and what you're doing here?"

He sat up and rubbed his pant legs. "Sure, sorry. My name is Peter Davis. I met you when I came—"

"You're that priest," I interrupted. "One of those priests who came down here during the time of the heated statue."

"I am. I'm surprised you remember me."

"Are you kiddin'? That story has become a legend around here. You've got to know slow towns love their ghost stories. I think it was your beard that threw me off." He rubbed and scratched at the brown fuzz gripping his face. "So I guess you did leave the priesthood, huh?" I asked, remembering what Walt had told me as I noticed Peter was not wearing his black suit and white collar.

"Not entirely," he answered. "I'm on sabbatical right now."

"What's that exactly mean for you?"

He chuckled. "I don't even know. That's just a word, really, but I guess you could say I'm taking a break of sorts. My vows are still intact and I'm technically still a priest, but I've been traveling, working a part-time job and doing some other things, trying to make sense of my life."

I recalled how Walt had lectured him and wondered if any of it had stuck. "Any sense been found?"

"Not sure." He stopped, dropped his head to the porch floor briefly before lifting it back up a second later. "I guess Walt told you what we talked about on your back porch if you knew I was thinking of leaving the priesthood."

"He told me some of it."

"I guess that's kind of why I'm here. I didn't handle that situation right. I was rude to Walt, even when he was trying to help me."

"*Did* he help you?"

Peter seemed surprised by the question, like it was the first time he had considered it. "Yes, I think he did. He had a simple way of explaining things that put it all in perspective. And I really admired him for taking the time to speak with me. He didn't have to do that. I was just a stranger."

"That's Walt," I replied, a hint of pride in my voice for being his friend. "So what have you been doing since you began this break of yours?"

"All types of things," Peter answered as he rose from his rocker and walked to the edge of the porch. He stuffed his hands in his pockets and studied the ocean horizon. "I've worked a part-time job at a port in New York City, but mostly I've been going to a lot of seminars and workshops meant to help priests struggling with their calling. I've also taken some religious theology classes and studied things, trying to rediscover why I originally became a priest. I'll have to admit, it's been a nice break."

"When is this little break of yours over?"

"This coming weekend," he answered. "If I don't report

back to Worcester by Monday, I have to leave the priesthood for good."

"I take it since you're saying 'if', you hadn't decided yet." Peter didn't respond or turn around. I decided to get up and join him as he watched the crashing waves. "So, did you come all the way down here from New York City *just* to see Walt?"

"No, not quite. I signed myself up for a workshop being given down the road in Charleston. It has an interesting speaker I've been wanting to hear."

I couldn't help but chuckle, which brought his gaze to me for the first time in minutes.

"Why are you laughing?"

"Charleston is an hour down the road, Peter. That's too far for a casual stop-off in Edisto. You sure there's not another reason you're here?"

Peter shrugged. "I'm not really sure why I'm here, Buck, if I'm being honest. But I'll admit I did go out of my way to find a reason to come down here. This break has helped a lot, but I've been getting pretty antsy about going back to the life I left. I'm not really as confident as I'd like to be about returning."

Sam got up from his spot on the dusty, porch floor and nudged at Peter's hand as it rested inside his pocket, much like he did to Walt when he wanted attention. Peter bent down and rubbed the dog's belly.

"I guess I maybe came out here to thank Walt," Peter said, standing back up and refocusing his attention on me, "for taking an interest in my life. I know he probably hasn't thought much about me since that day I left Edisto, but there were a few things he said that I haven't been able to stop thinking about, one in particular more than the others."

"What's that?"

Peter hesitated. "Walt mentioned this little girl in Costa Rica he helped out, or sponsored, I guess I should say, through his church."

"Sure. I remember him talking about her. What's got your interest about her?"

"I didn't tell Walt this, but last year I went to Costa Rica myself and met an orphaned girl there who melted my heart. She had the saddest story, but I felt so helpless because there was nothing I could do to help her. It was actually seeing her that brought back a lot of things from my past, things I thought I had buried."

"Walt said he felt helpless, too, when he spoke about his little girl; said he felt like his letters and the small amount of money he sent down there didn't do enough. But I'm afraid I still don't get why you're bringing up these two little girls."

"Well, I guess I'm wondering if it's only one little girl."

It took me a second to piece together what Peter was trying to say. "You think the one you met is the same one Walt's been helping?"

"Sounds crazy when you say it out loud, doesn't it?"

"Sure does. That's a decent sized country down there with a lot of little girls." Peter's face dropped. "But that sure as heck doesn't mean what you wonderin' can't be true. It could be the same child."

"Thanks, Buck. I don't know; I was just trying to make sense of that whole phenomenon with the statues. That little girl was the only connection I could find, with me meeting her and thinking so much about her, and then Walt mentioning her."

A breeze floated by and rattled the gutters of Walt's back porch. At the same moment, something rattled loose in my brain.

"Wait a minute! Would you recognize her if you saw her?"

"Sure," Peter responded, surprised by my question. "I think so."

"Walt had a picture of her. It used to sit on a table in his den."

We were both unable to move, until Sam barked and startled us into action. I pulled Walt's screen door open and raced inside. Peter followed with nervous footsteps while Sam galloped in behind him. I had packed up most of Walt's things in the last week, leaving the house empty save for a few boxes. In the back bedroom I began to plunge through the array of boxes while Peter and Sam paced behind me. It seemed no one would say anything until we had settled this matter. Finally, I found the one I was looking for. I ripped open the box labeled "Photos" and sifted through it as fast as I could. One of the pictures near the top was a framed snapshot of Olivia.

"Who is that?" Peter asked.

"That was Walt's wife. She died a long time ago. I think this was taken just before she passed away."

"Can I see it?" I handed it to Peter and was surprised by the way his eyes fell into the picture. "She was beautiful," he said as he handed the framed picture back to me.

I went back to digging through the box. "Here it is!" I shouted. When I handed it to Peter and saw his reaction, I already knew. "It's her, isn't it? That's the one you met."

Peter lifted his hand to his mouth, stumbled forward and sat down next to me on the creaking floorboards.

"This is amazing," I said.

"But what does it all mean? How are we supposed to make sense of this?" I shrugged. "Were the heated statues all about this little girl?"

"I suppose they were," I agreed, though I truly had no idea. "Maybe you're meant to go back and find her."

"But it seems there should be more to this. I understand God wanting to help a poor, orphaned child, but why me and Walt? What's the connection between us?"

I shook my head. "I wish I had an answer, Peter. I really do."

I heaved the box of pictures onto my lap and began flipping through the rest of them, mainly to relieve my nervous energy. My face warmed with pleasant memories as I saw a few of Walt and me.

Suddenly, Peter grabbed my wrist.

"Let me see that picture!"

He startled me terribly, but I handed him another framed picture as he set the one of the little girl down on the floor. He stared at the new picture for what felt like an eternity.

"How does Walt know her?"

I fumbled a question in return. "How do *you* know her?"

"Just answer me. How does he know Sister Marie? Why does Walt have a framed picture of her?"

My thoughts raced back through the weekend trip I had taken to Atlanta. "Well, I gave him this picture, actually. A while back I went to a children's home outside Atlanta and met her, met that nun. I was attempting to track down Walt's son. See, it's a long story, Peter, but Walt had a son he gave up a long time ago. I'd be happy to tell you about it, but—"

"I grew up at that orphanage," Peter interrupted.

"What?"

"Sister Marie was like a mother to me. She raised me at this orphanage for the first ten years of my life."

Neither of us could speak or move. Then suddenly, Sam barked again.

* * *

I could say with great certainty that Walt had left me about four days ago, even though his worn body still lay on a white, hospital bed. He told me in a weary voice about a dream he had some nights ago. It was a strange dream, one that had me thinking Walt had lost his wits for good. At the time, I felt sorry for him.

Now, I could only admire his faith.

Before climbing in my car to head to the hospital, Peter and I spent almost an hour exchanging stories. He told me about growing up at the orphanage with Sister Marie and the abusive parents who'd adopted him after his tenth birthday. I told him about Olivia dying in childbirth and the guilt Walt felt for walking out of that hospital without his son. I also told Peter about Walt's morning ritual, and what he prayed for each day after he finished playing his violin. After that, Peter cried, and I held him.

Most of the nurses and doctors on Walt's floor had come to know me. They called me by name as we passed, but they didn't know the bearded man by my side. "Why don't you let me go in first," I said to Peter. I put my arm around his trembling shoulders. "You okay with that?"

He nodded.

I slowly opened Walt's door and walked into the room. The cloth chair that had been my companion for the last few weeks was still perched to the left of the bed, with my favorite quilt laid on top of it, one my mother had sewed for me when I was a child. Tubes, charts, machines, and monitors surrounded Walt, all doing their best to prolong his life. I once heard a friend of mine say that he never understood why we spent so much time and money to keep elderly people alive for as long as we could. "What's the point?" he used to say. When he said this, my instinct was to tell him that it was our duty to protect human life as much as we could, and from there, it was in God's hands. In seeing how Walt's life had unfolded, I discovered I was right. Walt's destiny was to make it through these last few days. Only now did I understand why.

"Walt?"

I gently grabbed his hand. His skin was tough, like a rock worn down by the wind and the earth's soil. He groaned but didn't open his eyes. "I know you can hear me, buddy, so I'm going to tell you something now."

I gathered myself.

"I hope you still remember that dream you had the other night, the one where that beautiful angel came to you. She delivered you a message on that golden beach with the purple sea, said you'd meet your son before meeting your wife again. You remember that?"

Walt tilted his head over on his pillow and opened his eyelids just slightly. I could tell lifting them was as painful as anything he'd ever been through. "I didn't know what to think of that dream at the time," I continued, "and frankly, I had forgotten about it. But, well, there's someone here to see you, Walt." I turned around and waved to Peter, who stood outside the glass door like a child about to enter a mysterious dream. He walked into the room as I backed away from the bed.

"Walt, this is—"

"My son."

It was as clear as Walt's voice had been in weeks.

"Come Peter, please." Walt motioned Peter over to the bed. He took several heavy footsteps forward, sat in the chair and grabbed the metal railing bracing the bed.

"Have you," Walt began before having to stop and cough, "have you learned about your mother? And what happened when . . ."

Peter stopped him. "Buck told me. I know what happened the day I was born."

Walt closed his eyes and licked his cracked lips before responding. "Your mother loved you, boy. She loved you so much she gave up her life for you. Before she'd even laid her hazel eyes upon your tiny face, she was willing to take the risk to give you life. That's the kind of love only a mother knows. She was a good woman, Peter."

Peter gripped the railing tightly. "I understand. I wish I could have met her. I wish I hadn't . . . . I wish I hadn't done what I did to her."

Walt immediately waved his hand in Peter's face, but couldn't respond before spitting up blood and mucus into a white bowl by his bed. "That's not for you to say," Walt said after collecting himself. "Only one sin occurred in our family that day. There's nothin' I can say to atone for what I did, but

I need to look you in the eye and tell you how sorry I am for abandoning you."

Peter's head fell toward the floor.

"I lived everyday in devotion to praying for you," Walt went on, "trying to make up for my sins. But selfishly, I prayed mostly that this day would eventually come, the day where I could see you. There's nothing I can do for you now, and I've accepted that. But I hope you see that your suffering wasn't God's doing. It was caused by this man right here. Me. God didn't cause it. He fixed it. He found a way to lead you to a better life, and he gave me the blessing of seeing how fine you turned out despite the decision I made."

He paused for a breath and energy before continuing. "Our lives played out this way for a reason." Walt coughed again and lunged forward. Peter grabbed him and patted his back, trying to beat out the illness destroying his father's insides. Once Walt had recovered, he grabbed Peter's hand. "Somehow, those two statues brought us together. We didn't know at the time what we were to each other, but the Good Lord had us taken care of all along. Life's like that. We never see a blessing in the present, only when we look back on our past."

"But I doubted," Peter said with watery eyes. "I doubted everything. Why do I deserve to be a part of this, to see this miracle? How could I possibly deserve to stand before God?"

Walt shook his head and reached up to the oxygen tubes in his nose. Peter and I tried to stop him, but Walt had somehow regained his strength for a brief instant. He pushed us away with the power of a young man and motioned to let him be as he pulled out the tubes. Peter sat back down in the chair as I returned to my place at the foot of the bed.

"God works on us all in different ways," Walt said after a long pause, "don't continue to drift away because of shame, son. You felt cursed all this time, I know, and you were frustrated with God. But sometimes it's those of us who suffer the most who are closest to Him. Please see now that you were actually blessed. God chose *you* for this miracle. He must want to use you in some way. God always has a purpose, even if that purpose takes a lifetime to show itself. You must go live your life, Peter, and please forgive me, so that I can let go of mine."

Peter tried to speak, but faltered. I think in a way, he didn't fully comprehend what was happening. The only reason Walt understood everything so clearly was because he had begun to pass into another life, a life that takes away your physical abilities, but somehow gives you the capability to see the world the way God intends us to see it.

I wanted so badly for Peter to forgive his father, for Walt to hear the words he had waited to hear for almost forty years. But still, Peter remained silent. His eyes stayed drawn to the floor. Perhaps his silence came from shame at what he had doubted; perhaps from anger toward Walt; perhaps from the overwhelming feeling of meeting his father for the first time. But whatever the reason, several deep breaths were all he could manage. Walt eventually broke the silence.

"Buck?"

"Yeah," I said, approaching his bedside.

"I've said my piece, and I thank God that Peter's heard it. But this isn't where I want to go. I want to be as close to her as possible."

I nodded. I went and spoke with the doctors and nurses, doing my best to convince them that they needed to look past their rules and regulations this one time. Walt knew his end was here, and they had no chance in stopping that. Didn't much matter anyway; I intended to take Walt home no matter what they said.

Peter and I lifted him from the bed as gently as we could. His body was feeble, his bones as soft as tissue paper and his hair all but gone. We placed him in a wheel chair and pushed him to my car. There wasn't much said between the three of us on the drive home. I knew Walt wanted to say goodbye to Edisto as we drove through the quiet streets and past the grand oaks. This place had become his refuge in the last thirty some years. The glorious sunrises, gentle sea breezes, and sandy beaches of Edisto were all dear friends who had helped Walt live with the pain of his past decisions.

When we reached Walt's home, I pulled into the gravel driveway. Peter and I braced Walt as best we could as he got out of the passenger seat. His body was fading with each passing second. The three of us walked around the house, over the sand and grass. Peter held onto Walt's right arm, and I the left. I wondered where Sam was, knowing Walt would want to see him, but he was already sitting on the beach, waiting on his master with a wagging tail.

All those mornings Walt sat on this beach as the sun rose from beyond the water, but on that day the sun was setting behind us, tinting the sky with shades of orange and violet. A pack of pelicans flew by above us in a perfect V-shape, gliding peacefully with a wind gust that took them out to sea.

"Did you give Olivia my violin?" Walt asked me.

"I did, buddy. She took it with open arms."

When we reached the edge of the beach and the end of Walt's backyard, I decided my part in this was up.

"You take him from here, Peter. Out there is where he played for your mother each morning, hoping she'd bring you to him. Now that you're here, I don't think it's fitting for me to be down there with y'all."

I let go of Walt's arm, but before we separated, he squeezed my hand. He wouldn't look at me, nor could I look at him. Old men aren't supposed to cry, even old saps like us.

When walking proved too difficult for Walt, Peter lifted his father into his arms and carried him down the beach, toward the falling waves and scattered seashells. It took them several minutes to reach Sam. When they got there, Peter laid Walt on the sand, then sat next to him. Sam licked Walt on the face before backing away and sitting down too, all three of them facing the ocean waters.

I wanted to be down there with Walt for his last seconds, but this was a family moment for the Henderson's. Walt, Olivia, Peter and Sam III were the only ones there on that sandy beach in Edisto, and I think that's the way God intended it to be. But luckily, there came a sea breeze just then, one that carried a message with it. From my perch near Walt's back porch, I heard Peter forgive his father as he held him tightly.

A moment later, Walt laid his head on his son's shoulder, departing for the other side of the ocean's horizon in the currents of a violin's melody.

26

September 5th, 1995

I, FATHER Paul Moore, stand now in the back of this small, stone church, preparing myself to help celebrate a Mass honoring the miracle that took place here three years ago. It is a glorious day in this New England harbor town. The autumn breeze swirls pleasantly amidst the changing leaves and over the rocky, ocean waters as the parishioners of Our Lady of the Sea file into their church. Word has spread about the story of Walter Henderson being reunited with his son, Father Peter Davis Henderson, through the miracle of the Virgin statues. To honor what took place here, we will celebrate this Mass, offering thanks for the intercession of the Divine. On opposite years, the Mass will be held down south on Edisto Island, South Carolina, the sister parish that will always and forever be associated with this church in Jamestown.

To begin the Mass, I walk up the center aisle alongside Peter and behind a slew of altar boys and other priests. The choir sings Ave Maria behind us, a song that brings purity to all voices. Though I try to remain focused, I can't help letting my eyes slide across each pew, taking note of the many souls this event has touched.

Buck Washington, as true a Southern gentleman as there ever was, sits in the front right pew draped in his Sunday best. In his eyes, I can see he is tired. His failing health almost kept him from making it to this ceremony, but I knew he wouldn't have missed it for anything. Some men's hearts are made only for kindness, and Buck is one of these men. He was the one who brought Walt's son to him in the end. Without Buck, this day may never have happened.

Sitting close to Buck is a woman I hadn't encountered before today, but I feel like I've known her my whole life. Sister Marie is approaching one hundred years of age, but still chugs along with just as much energy as one of the many toddlers she helped raise. I often heard Peter say that there is no way he could ever repay this woman, and I'm sure Walt feels the same way. Sister Marie received Peter with open arms when she could have said no, much like the Virgin Mary received our Lord two millennia ago.

In one of the other front pews sits a young man of nearly twenty-five, but his innocence is that of a child's. Donald Devonshire has sat in this church more than anyone else here today. His grandmother rests to his right, the two of them holding hands. I have often asked the Virgin Mary in my prayers why she chose Donald as her soul to communicate with. Although I have yet to hear an answer, I feel one of my original assumptions could have been accurate. It *is* true that the mentally challenged are the most like her Son, so I know she keeps a special eye on them, perhaps more so than all the rest of us. Donald will never let unhappiness find him, mainly because of the trust he has in his heart. There will be things he doesn't have answers to, just like the rest of us, but Donald knows someone above him does have the answers, and that should give us all comfort if only we would trust like he does. "Why do you need to know when she knows for you?" he had asked us that day. I can only pray that I one day have the faith Donald has. He waves to me from his seat, excited by the love that fills his church today, a church which he keeps so neat and tidy. I suppose he is also excited for the Celtics game Peter and I promised to take him to next month. We got him seats right behind the bench, where he'll no doubt be wearing his green headband.

There are many others amongst the congregation, even some who have been absent between these walls in the past, including a hard-nosed fire Sergeant, sitting quietly up front with his arm clutching his wife's shoulders. But only one other in particular controls my gaze; a little girl with brown complexion and flowing, dark hair. She's new to this part of the world, noticed by her shy nature and broken speech. This little girl has begun a new life here, leaving a past of suffering behind. She has Peter to thank for that. He tracked her down from a brief meeting they shared years ago in a small, poverty-stricken village in Costa Rica. Peter has found her a loving home with a lonely widow who was never able to have children of her own. As Juliet O'Day holds the hand of this little girl, it is clear that the two of them will bring joy to one another.

In the midst of all that happened, there is one thing that touched my heart more than anything else. I learned that Walter Henderson played his violin on the beach each morning for his deceased wife. He played as the sun rose from beyond the water, knowing she was up in heaven listening. Through his musical notes, he spoke to God, weaving his whispered prayers into the music and asking that his lost son be brought back to him. Although the statues only warmed the earth for a matter of days, it was Walt's unrelenting faith that endured for almost half a century. His failures as a man brought sadness into this world, but Walt's story proves that God has the ability to heal that sadness, if only we would allow his providential grace to take hold of our lives.

All those mornings Walt sat playing his violin on the beach, he hoped his music would lead Peter to him. But as I watch Peter begin the Mass from behind the altar, I realize Walt must no longer play his songs, for the music of the angels soaring all around him will one day bring his son home to him once more.

CPSIA information can be obtained at www.ICGtesting.com
Printed in the USA
BVOW071408291112

306765BV00001B/2/P